"You believe all of that business about there being a true love for everyone? Or is it just for your show?"

Funny, but no one else had ever asked Ashley that question. "I do believe it."

Marcus took a look around the dance floor. All eyes on them. "I'm tempted to give them a show."

His rich, buttery accent was working its way into her. "What did you have in mind?"

"If we do it, I think we start slowly, give them a taste of what's to come."

"Of course. We wouldn't want to go too fast." Except that she was thinking about nothing but going very fast, away from this party, away with him.

"I could start by kissing your cheek, whispering in your ear that you look beautiful tonight." He did exactly that as he said it, his warm lips on her face, his hot breath against her ear, skimming the slope of her neck.

Finally. A kiss. His approach was commanding and entirely self-assured, his grasp on her so firm—she wasn't sure she'd ever been kissed so masterfully.

When they came up for air, her head was in the clouds. Flashes of light surrounded them. So this was what it was like to see fireworks.

Sep 16

Dear Reader,

Full disclosure: I have a thing for British men. It started with James Bond when I was a girl. Duran Duran came along when I was a teenager, and that sealed the deal. It's the way they carry themselves, the dry (and often naughty) sense of humor and, of course, the accent.

The CEO Daddy Next Door has a British hero— hard-nosed and handsome single dad Marcus Chambers, who is in the US temporarily. He moves in next door to determined, but slightly scattered, reality-TV matchmaker Ashley George. Her life and apartment renovation are intruding on Marcus's peace and quiet. He's not a fan, however gorgeous she is.

These two were so much fun to write. They were an endless source of sexy banter and restrained flirtation. One of my favorite scenes comes after their first kiss. Ashley is reeling and unsure where this is going. Marcus has a young daughter, and that responsibility terrifies her. Still, she has to test the waters. She offers him her hand in the back of the limo on the way home after a party. But Marcus doesn't take her hand. He doesn't kiss her. He's too torn over his attraction to a woman he isn't sure is good for him. Instead, he surprises both Ashley and himself with a sweet story that turns to seduction, employing nothing more than his fingertip on her palm and his buttery British accent. Marcus melts the page...and Ashley. I hope you find it just as sexy!

Happy reading!

Karen

KAREN BOOTH

THE CEO DADDY NEXT DOOR

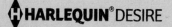

HARLEQUIN® DESIRE

Recycling programs
for this product may
not exist in your area.

ISBN-13: 978-0-373-73478-8

The CEO Daddy Next Door

Printed in U.S.A.

Karen Booth is a Midwestern girl transplanted in the South, raised on '80s music, Judy Blume and the films of John Hughes. She loves to write big-city love stories. When she takes a break from the art of romance, she's teaching her kids about good music, honing her Southern cooking skills or sweet-talking her astoundingly supportive husband into mixing up a cocktail. You can find out more about Karen or contact her at karenbooth.net.

Books by Karen Booth

Harlequin Desire

That Night with the CEO
Pregnant by the Rival CEO
The CEO Daddy Next Door

Visit her Author Profile page at Harlequin.com, or karenbooth.net, for more titles.

For my amazing friend and long-lost sister, Piper Trace. You helped me get through this book and I'm forever grateful. May we have years of giggly brainstorming sessions ahead of us.

One

Pure exasperation rushed from Ashley George's lips when she closed her apartment door and spotted Marcus Chambers waiting for the elevator.

"I suppose you'd like me to hold the lift." Marcus's rich British accent and unflinching delivery made the statement far more annoying. He knew she was headed downstairs. Unless she was going to descend eleven flights of their Manhattan apartment building in under five minutes while wearing a pencil skirt and four-inch heels, she'd need the elevator.

She sucked in a deep breath and breezed past him as she stepped onboard. Her long blond locks were given a swish for good measure.

"First floor?" he asked.

She dug her fingernails into her palms. Two seconds in the same space and he was already on her last nerve. "We both know we're going to the same meeting. Being cute about it won't help."

He straightened the jacket of his charcoal-gray suit, folded his hands before him and looked straight ahead at the doors. "A gentleman is never cute."

Cute was definitely an undersell in Marcus Chambers's case. Ridiculously handsome, yes. Which was too bad, because he was also a grump of epic proportions. Whatever made him that way had to be genetics or a product of his past. Otherwise, he seemed to have everything—money, a primo apartment at a prestigious address on the Upper West Side, enough good looks for a lifetime and—although Ashley had seen Lila only in passing—a beautiful baby girl.

"I wouldn't be in this elevator at all if you'd stop complaining to the building board," Ashley replied.

He cleared his throat. "And I wouldn't have to complain if you'd hire a competent contractor to finish your renovations. I'm tired of living in chaos." He glanced over his shoulder and dismissed her with a flash of his piercing green eyes. "Chaos seems to follow you wherever you go."

Ashley pursed her lips. He wasn't entirely wrong. Considering the things he'd witnessed, her life probably looked like a tornado with nine lives. She was always in a rush, often juggling her phone while many of the million things going through her head managed to leak out of her mouth. Sure, there had been problems with the renovations to her apartment. Sometimes things didn't go smoothly. She did her best to keep things on track and really, he hadn't even tried to be more understanding.

She sighed and leaned against the elevator wall, stealing another eyeful of him. If he underwent a personality transplant or at least learned to take a deep breath, he might be perfect—strong jaw with a devilishly square chin, close-cut scruff along his jaw, thick head of mahogany brown hair. Her vision dipped lower and she shuddered as images of his glorious chest and astounding abs flashed in her head. She hadn't been lucky enough to see his torso live and in person, but she'd unearthed photos of him on the internet. He was one of Britain's most eligible bachelors, as billed in a charity calendar full of hunky guys. A bachelor raising a baby—divorce was a terrible thing.

Somewhere in the world was a true match for this stunning-on-the-outside, stodgy-on-the-inside man. Ashley believed that about everyone. It wasn't a made-for-TV act she put on for her reality show, her namesake, *Manhattan Matchmaker*. True love and soul mates were real, just as real as the things in life everyone feared—broken hearts, family illnesses, life-or-death obligations.

Ashley still believed she'd find her own match someday, but after getting dumped before Thanksgiving by the guy she'd thought was "the one," she'd decided to take a year off from dating. Focus on herself in the context of "me," not "we." She hadn't lasted long. Marcus had moved in during the first few days of January, he asked her out a week after they'd met, and she'd stupidly said yes. That night three months ago had done nothing but prove her thesis: she had no business being with a man right now. She didn't trust her instincts when it came to love, at least not where her own heart was concerned. Not after the heartbreak of James. And her life was indeed chaos.

Marcus moved his head to the side as if working out a kink in his neck. A waft of his aftershave settled on her, its effect on her as unavoidable as the heat of a South Carolina summer. *Damn.* He even smelled good—warm and masculine, just like the finest bourbon, peculiar since Marcus was CEO of his family-owned gin distillery.

The elevator dinged. "After you." His velvety accent echoed in her head. If only he'd used it for something along the lines of, "Don't you look smashing? I'm sorry I've been such an ass the last three months."

Ashley strode down the hall. Her skirt was too tight to take the extralong strides she hoped could convey her determination to come out of this confab unscathed, but she still marched into the meeting room, stilted gait and all. The five members of the building's board sat at a long table, conferring. Ashley's stomach lurched when she saw the board president, Tabitha Townsend. Tabitha regarded Ashley as if she were a red wine spill on white carpet. Ashley wasn't exactly about to invite her over for cosmos and girl talk. And now it was time to charm Tabitha and the board, when Ashley had just had an exhausting day of publicity for the new season of *Manhattan Matchmaker.*

"Hello, everyone." Ashley shook hands with her only ally, Mrs. White, a longtime building resident. She was not only upper-crust through and through but also a reality TV addict. Ashley's show was one of her favorites.

"Will you say it for me? Just once?" Mrs. White asked, looking hopeful.

Ashley didn't have a choice. She had to make *somebody* in this room happy. "I'm Ashley George, and I find true love in the city that never sleeps."

Mrs. White clapped her hands together in glee. "I love it when you do that. I brag to all my friends about it."

"Anytime for you," Ashley replied.

The corners of Mrs. White's mouth turned down. "I only wish tonight's meeting was under better circumstances. We should be talking about the new season of your show, not neighborly squabbles."

"I assure you, they're more than squabbles," Marcus interjected with all the warmth of an iceberg.

Mrs. White shook her head, eyes darting back and forth between them. "It's a shame, you know. You two would make a lovely couple. Have you ever thought about that? Going out to dinner to work out your differences?"

Marcus huffed. Oh, they'd been out to dinner, and it had gone horribly. Nervous to a fault, Ashley had one too many glasses of wine before the appetizers arrived. Apparently she hadn't fully processed her breakup with James because she rambled on and on about it, about how he'd dumped her because she cared too much about her career, because she wasn't ready to commit, wasn't ready to have kids. The list of reasons she'd been rejected was long. Marcus had reacted to it so badly that the night ended with a handshake. That had been a major disappointment... It wasn't like she'd been foolish enough to think she and Marcus Chambers would fall in love, but he was such a hottie. She'd been looking forward to a kiss.

Her renovation project started the next day. Thus the battle of Chambers vs. George, a fight she wished would die, was born.

"Careful, or people will start to think you're the matchmaker." Ashley held on to Mrs. White's hand, wanting to stay with the one person in the room who was on her side.

She eventually moved along, arriving at Tabitha, who didn't offer her hand but rather a stabbing glare. Luckily she turned, and her eyes landed on Marcus. "Mr. Chambers. It's nice to see you this evening." She ran her manicured fingers along the neckline of her blouse. Despite her attempt at being alluring, Tabitha was definitely not Marcus's perfect match. Anyone could see that. He belonged with a woman carved from marble, not one made of fire and brimstone. "Take a seat, Ms. George," Tabitha snapped.

Ashley twisted her lips but followed orders, perching in one of two chairs facing the table. This wasn't quite the setup for an HOA meeting. It was more a firing squad, especially given Tabitha's presence. Ashley crossed her legs, setting her handbag on the floor. Marcus took the seat next to hers.

"Ms. George," Tabitha began. "It's apparent to the board that your apartment renovation is out of control."

Off to a great start. Ashley squirmed in her seat.

Tabitha opened a thick folder overflowing with papers. Marcus had been thorough with his complaints. "Your workers, and in particular the foreman, have little regard for the only other tenant of your floor, Mr. Chambers. There have been circular saws at seven in the morning…"

"I was out of town," Ashley interjected. "I'm sorry that happened."

"Ms. George. Please raise your hand before speaking." Tabitha flipped to the next page. "There has been loud music of some sort…"

Ashley thrust her hand into the air. "It's just pop music, and the carpenters love it. If you'd just let me explain…"

"I'm not finished, Ms. George. Quiet. Please."

Ashley slumped back in her chair. "Sorry."

Tabitha cleared her throat. "As I was saying, the workers have repeatedly made a mess in the hall you share with Mr. Chambers, tracking drywall dust and dirt. They don't clean up after themselves, and worst of all, they have been seen smoking in the building, which is a fire hazard and strictly prohibited."

Ashley's stomach turned. The most tragic event of her entire life had been a fire. "They know they're not supposed to do that. I've told them. I'll tell them again."

"Frankly, I'm tempted to tell you right now that you must halt the project and hire another contractor."

Ashley's queasiness became nearly unbearable. She'd been on this contractor's waiting list for a year, and they were her second choice. The wait for her first choice was closer to eighteen months, and that time frame was given to her *after* she'd pulled celebrity strings. The contractor she'd hired did solid work affordably, an absolute necessity with her sizable obligations to her family back in South Carolina.

She couldn't put the project on hold. She'd lose every penny she'd paid the contractor up front. It would take months to recover from that financially, and she'd be stuck living in a construction zone when her entire aim this year was to make her life more stable. With her work schedule and her father's worsening health after several strokes, visions of Ashley's dream apartment were the only thing that kept her going some days. She'd come from nothing and she'd worked damn hard for this apartment. She wasn't about to let that slip between her fingers.

"I'm very sorry if this has been an inconvenience to Mr. Chambers. I'll speak to the builder and let him know how serious this is. We'll get it straightened out this time."

Tabitha shook her head. "After reviewing the file, the board has determined that this time is the last time, Ms. George. If your project can't be completed in a manner Mr. Chambers finds acceptable, we're pulling the plug. One more complaint from him and you're done."

Ashley's eyes darted to Marcus. The corners of his mouth were twitching. Was he actually going to smile? "One more complaint? You've got to be kidding me." She tossed her hand in his direction. "There's no pleasing him. He probably has a complaint about the way I'm sitting in this chair. This is completely unfair."

Completely unfair. Apt words considering Ms. George's willingness to ignore the disruptions of her apartment renovations. Marcus and his eleven-month-old daughter, Lila, were trying to carve out a new life for themselves in New York. It was only fair that he deliver the final blow if the mayhem continued.

"Mr. Chambers," Mrs. White interjected from her end of the table. "Please understand the seriousness of this situation. We don't want to be forced to shut down Ms. George's project for something minor."

"Thank you," Ashley blurted, with a strain of desperation. "The scales can't be tipped entirely in his favor. If you put him in control, my project will be shut down before we get back upstairs."

Marcus reared back his head. Why was she acting as though he was the unreasonable one? This mess was of her making, and she'd dismissed it at every turn. "You act as if I'm making a big deal out of this."

"I said I was sorry."

Tabitha rubbed her forehead. "The board will not reverse the decision. One more complaint from Mr. Chambers and Ms. George must hire a new contractor."

"But…" Ashley slipped.

"Not another word, Ms. George." Tabitha delivered a look so stern even Marcus was rubbed the wrong way by it.

A moment of heavy, uncomfortable quiet played out. Ashley shifted in her seat, and his eyes drifted to her leg. More specifically, the stretch of her shapely calf and delicate ankle, punctuated by a gleaming black patent leather stiletto pump. He didn't have many weaknesses, but he did have a soft spot a mile wide for a woman in sexy shoes. The fact that Ashley was wearing those shoes... If anything was unfair at that particular moment, that might have been it. He forced himself to look away. Ashley's beauty, her pull on him, made her a woman to be kept at arm's length. It was the only way to keep his head straight.

Mrs. White cleared her throat. "I'd like to add one stipulation. Mr. Chambers should have to take any complaint to Ms. George first. Please try to work it out."

Marcus blinked several times. *Deal directly with Ms. George?* Oh no. That wasn't going to work for him at all. "You can't be serious. She's clearly demonstrated tonight that she'll argue any complaint forever. How am I supposed to work anything out with her?"

"I can be reasonable."

"Because you have such a great track record with that sort of behavior?" Marcus asked, his pulse choosing an offbeat rhythm.

Tabitha dismissed them with a flutter of her hands. "Mrs. White is right. Work it out."

Marcus and Ashley filed out of the room as if they

were two children who'd been sent to their rooms without a proper supper. Neither could claim a true victory, but at least Marcus had the upper hand. He was thankful for that. When the lift doors opened, he held them for Ashley.

"I need to make sure I have all of your phone numbers," she said curtly. "Your office. The home number. In case there's a problem."

He fished his cell phone from his pocket, choking back the words he wanted to say. There already was a problem. After their one date, he'd promised himself that he would stay as far away from her as possible. Ashley represented his most selfish tendencies, the part of him that craved a woman who was untamed and brimming with life, gorgeous and sexy and just a little bit crazy. His priority was finding a mother for Lila, and that meant a woman who was sensible and calm, and who acted in an entirely predictable way. He could learn to live with that, for Lila.

Ashley rested her enormous handbag on her knee and bent over it, rummaging through the contents. Marcus tried to avert his eyes, but he couldn't. They were drawn to her cleavage the way a man roaming a desert is drawn to cool water. His breath caught in his throat. Her skin was a delicate wash of peach and pink, curving, dipping and swelling. A lock of her golden-blond hair fell from her shoulders, draping across her gorgeous display. His eyes clamped shut. He couldn't take another minute. Ashley was the thorn in his side, however much she might resemble the rose that grew alongside it.

The elevator dinged, the doors slid open and they came face-to-face with the only person to improve his mood reliably—Lila.

Lila's nanny, Catherine, was pushing her in the stroller. "Mr. Chambers. I was about to take Lila out for a short walk before bed." Catherine's wide eyes were glued to Ashley. "Ms. George. I loved last night's *Manhattan Matchmaker*."

"Please, call me Ashley. And it was just a rerun, wasn't it?" Ashley stepped out into the hall.

Catherine seemed as if she might burst from excitement. She was so taken with Ashley and her show. It was all she and his housekeeper, Martha, seemed to talk about, which drove Marcus crazy. He could see why people might be beguiled by her, but the show itself was silly. A ruse. True love. Soul mates. Fiction.

"But I love that episode," Catherine said. "It was the one with the doctor and the woman who owns the bakery. Only you could've put those two people together. They totally fell in love."

Ashley smiled. "That's very sweet of you to say. Thank you."

Marcus held the elevator while Catherine pushed the stroller onboard and turned it around. Marcus leaned down to press a kiss to Lila's forehead, inhaling the sweet scent that came from her wispy blond hair. He rubbed his thumb across her rosy cheek. The smile and gurgle she gave him were salve for his soul. Without question, she was the most precious thing in his life, and she deserved so much more than he could give her on his own. Precisely the reason to avoid Ashley and find Lila a mum. "You have fun, my darling. Daddy will read you a bedtime story when you come home." He released the doors as Catherine waved goodbye.

"Your daughter is adorable. And very sweet. You know, that's only the second time I've seen her. I didn't even see her the night..." Ashley looked up at the ceiling for a moment. "You know. The night we went out. You've done a good job of keeping her from me."

I do a good job of keeping Lila from everyone. Protecting Lila was more than his charge. It was his strongest instinct. She'd been dealt a rotten hand in life, and it was his fault. He'd chosen the wrong woman for a wife and when things got bad, he'd convinced her that having a baby would make everything better. He was the reason Lila's mother wasn't there for her.

"I believe you were about to give me your other phone numbers," he said, changing the subject.

"I'll send you a text right now." Ashley punched away at the keyboard. "Then you'll have my info."

Marcus's phone lit up with the other numbers. And a message. *I'm not evil. Just so you know.*

"I never said you were evil, Ms. George."

"Please don't call me Ms. George. We've been on a date. It will make life much easier if we can drop the formalities."

"Very little in life is easy, but if that will placate you, I will call you Ashley."

Ashley narrowed her stare. For a moment, it was

as if she was peering down into his soul, and he didn't like that feeling at all. "You're grumpy before your time, Chambers. And I don't get it, because you weren't like that when I first met you. What exactly has made you such a curmudgeon?"

"I appreciate your deft use of the English language, but I hardly think this is an appropriate topic of conversation."

He turned for his door, but Ashley's hand on his arm stopped him. It was as if he was wearing no jacket at all. The warmth of her touch cut right through the wool. He looked down at her slender fingers curved around his biceps.

"You can't hide from things. You definitely can't hide from me. I'm a very perceptive person. That's why I have the job I do. I see things in people they don't see in themselves."

He turned his sights to her face, fighting the sensations coursing through his body. Warmth. Attraction. A deep, desperate desire to weave his fingers through her hair, cup the back of her head and claim the kiss he'd deprived himself of the night they went on their date. The look in her wide brown eyes was one of the most sincere he'd ever seen. It would've been so easy to give in to the way she made him feel at that instant. But he owed Lila too much. "Good night, Ms. George."

She shook her head and patted him on the shoulder. "It's Ashley, Chambers. You'll get it eventually."

Two

Ashley had given Marcus a slew of top-secret nicknames—Tower of London for his stature, the Earl of Handsome for obvious reasons and the British Pain-in-the-Butt, reserved for moments like last night. She had very few problems figuring out most people. Marcus was another case. Why did he dislike her so much? After her scolding at the HOA meeting, she'd spent much of the night trying to sort it out. She'd devoted most of the ride to her office that morning to thinking about it, too. The man had it all. So why be so unhappy? Why be so closed off?

A knock came at Ashley's office door. Grace from network publicity poked her head inside, her wavy auburn hair in a messy bun that only someone truly self-assured could pull off.

"You ready for me?" She didn't wait for an answer, breezing into Ashley's office in a tailored gray suit and heels. The benefit of having accepted the office space the network had offered was that meetings were a simple matter of strolling down the hall. The downside was being under their thumb.

Ashley nodded, untangling herself from confusing thoughts about Marcus. "Yes. Of course." She collected a stack of papers on her desk, turned to a clean page on a legal pad and picked up a pen. It was time to get to work. There were several final details to discuss for the *Manhattan Matchmaker* premiere party.

"So? Do I dare ask what happened with your building board meeting last night?" Grace took a chair opposite Ashley's desk, resting her laptop on her knees. Grace had been a champion of Ashley's show from the very beginning, and they'd become good friends over the three years they'd worked together.

"They decided that one more complaint from the Tower of London and I have to hire a new contractor."

Grace winced. "Ouch. Harsh."

"Tell me about it." The uneasy feeling in her stomach returned. Marcus had too much control over the one thing in her life that was strictly hers. "Bottom line? He hates me. That's pretty clear by now, and I can't get past the idea that it's about more than the mess in the hall."

"I can't fathom anyone hating you, Ash. It sounds to me like he's just an uptight guy. He shook your hand after a date. Who does that?"

"Don't remind me." Yet another piece of evidence

supporting her supposition. Marcus simply disliked her. "Let's just get to work. I have a million things to do before the party Thursday night. The people over at Peter Richie are going to strangle me if I don't show up for my final dress fitting this afternoon."

Grace shook her head in dismay. "Ash. Peter Richie is one of the hottest designers on the planet, he's giving you a dress for your party and you still haven't shown up for your final fitting? It's two days away."

"I know. I'm terrible." The truth was that she'd been avoiding it. Peter had been gracious and generous, but she was keenly aware that the Manhattan Matchmaker had been afforded the luxury, not the real Ashley George. A designer making a couture gown for her? Ludicrous. The real Ashley had grown up with dresses her mother had made.

Grace opened up her laptop. "If you haven't dealt with your dress, I don't even want to guess the status of you finding a date."

Ashley's lips twisted into a tight bunch. She'd been hoping the network would forget they'd made the request for her to find a date for the premiere party. "They're still insisting on this?"

"Yes. The premiere is a network function to publicize your show. And don't forget they still haven't given you an answer on the new show you pitched to them. You do not want to be anything less than a woman who says yes."

"They're just fixated on this because of those stupid gossip website photos."

"The image of you buying ice cream and a candy bar on a Saturday night did not help your image. And that affects the ratings."

"That was three weeks ago and I had the world's worst PMS. It has nothing to do with not having a boyfriend." Although if she'd had a boyfriend, she could have sent him out for the ice cream. "I hate the fact that anyone cares about this."

Grace began tapping away at her laptop. "And not just a little. You know it's the most popular topic on the *Manhattan Matchmaker* message boards. Your fans want to see you happy. They want to know that the woman who finds true love for everyone else can find it for herself. And the last time I checked, Ash, you live on this kind of attention."

Actually, Ashley didn't live on that kind of attention. She existed on it. She made money because of it. After she'd watched her parents struggle for years, working tirelessly and never getting ahead, it was nice to know she'd broken that particular family tradition.

Ashley sucked in a deep breath. "You're going to have to set me up with someone or call a male escort service. I have no prospects."

"No way. Word will get out if I try to arrange something. I can just see it in the papers." With a dramatic sweep of both hands, Grace made a nightmare materialize. "The Manhattan Matchmaker Can't Find Her Own Match."

"Hey. That's not fair. You know I'm intentionally taking a break from men."

"And my grandmother would say that you fall off the horse, you need to get right back on it."

"Yeah, well, my saddle is out of commission. I haven't even been on a real date since James broke up with me."

Grace's eyes flickered in a way that made Ashley squirm. "That's not true. The Tower of London? You've been on a date with him."

It felt as though Ashley's heart had seized up in her chest. "No. That was not a date. It was a disaster."

"He asked you out. That counts as a date." Grace scooted forward in her seat, her eyes brimming with entirely too much excitement. "Just think. If you get him to come to the party, it'll be that much harder for him to complain about your apartment."

"What about 'familiarity breeds contempt'?"

"Now you're just making excuses. What's his real name again? Marcus…" She glanced down at her computer and began typing.

"Chambers," Ashley grumbled. How exactly was this going to work? Oh, wait. It wouldn't. Marcus would say no, and that would make every hallway encounter excruciatingly miserable.

"Here he is." Grace nodded as she looked at her laptop screen, her eyes scanning back and forth. "Chambers Gin…famous British family…divorce." She looked up. "Divorce?"

"Yes. I told you that. Remember? He has a baby. Lila. I don't really know much other than his wife came from a prestigious family, too, and whatever happened between the two of them, she took off six weeks after the baby was born." Ashley rubbed her forehead. "It's all online if you read enough."

"I take it you've read it all."

"Pretty much. What can I say? I was curious. A ridiculously hot guy moves in across the hall, a girl Googles him."

"His wife leaves him and the baby six weeks after she's born? Whatever broke them up had to have been bad."

"Or it'd been brewing for a long time. The reason for the divorce was listed as 'irretrievable breakdown.' I guess that's what they call irreconcilable differences in the UK."

"Yeah, but a mother leaving her child?"

"I know. It's awful."

Grace returned her vision to the screen. "Financial markets… Cambridge University…"

"Will you just give this up? He's never going to agree to go with me to that party, anyway."

"Shush. I'm reading. Rowing team…yada yada yada. Oh. My. God." She clamped her hand over her mouth. Her eyes were as big as hubcaps when she looked up at Ashley.

She found it.

"He's in a calendar. Britain's most eligible bachelors."

"Oh yeah. That. Sorta funny, isn't it? I mean, Mr. November? I'd give him crap about it if I wasn't trying to keep him calm."

"So you've seen the pictures?"

She shrugged it off, pretending to busy herself

with her pen and pad. "It's not like I bought one of the calendars." Of course she hadn't. It was sold out.

"I can't believe you didn't tell me about this. We just hit the mother lode. This is perfect. You invite the hot British gin maker and I get to write the world's most amazing press release. This might end up being the pinnacle of my career."

"Oh please. It's a calendar to raise money for a children's hospital. They do it every year. I doubt it's a big deal."

"Uh, the picture of him with no shirt? I can guarantee people will care about that. A lot of people."

Grace got up from her chair, set her computer on Ashley's desk and flipped it around. They were both confronted with one of Britain's most eligible bachelors and his splendid physique. "You told me he was handsome, but you really undersold it. Look at his abs. And those shoulders."

Ashley shook her head, wishing she could erase the image of Marcus's incredible torso, the one lovingly embossed on her brain. *Is it stuffy in here?* "You're making a big deal out of nothing. That photo is probably airbrushed like crazy." With the computer on her desk, it was impossible to avoid shirtless, sweaty Marcus, standing on shore next to the River Thames after a rowing race, smiling no less. "And I mean, he might *look* hot, but ignore that. He can be insufferable if he wants to be."

"I could put up with a whole lot of insufferable for a guy with abs like that." Grace returned to her seat, thankfully removing the influence of the pictures.

"The network is going to be over the moon when I tell them you're bringing one of Britain's most eligible bachelors to the premiere party."

"Hold on a second. I haven't even asked him. Were you not listening earlier? He hates me. Hates. Me."

Grace didn't react to Ashley's words, instead looking at her laptop screen. "It says here that he's responsible for the US launch of a whole new brand of gin for his family's distillery. That's not an inexpensive proposition. We can help him with that. Every entrepreneur loves free publicity."

And at what cost? Ashley's pride, that's what. The matchmaker truly couldn't find her own match. After her heart *and* her pride were destroyed by James, her avoidance of men was intentional, but temporary. At no point had it meant that she wasn't still hoping Mr. Right would turn up. Now she had to resort to bribing Mr. Not-Right-At-All, just to appease the network and save face.

"So, what are you waiting for? Call him. I'll wait until you're done before I start writing the press release."

It'd been high school since Ashley had asked out a guy, and that hadn't gone well. Suddenly her hands were clammy. She certainly wasn't afraid of Marcus. But she *was* afraid he'd say no.

"I don't need to tell you the gravity of the situation." Marcus's father's voice was unusually cold. It was the tinny overseas connection on speakerphone, Marcus hoped. He couldn't stand the thought of his normally cheerful dad being so gravely unhappy. "If we can't get this endeavor of yours off the ground, the ramifications will be great. It's not just the loss of expected growth. It's the money we've put into it, as well. It has to work."

Yes, it does. Marcus looked across the conference table at his sister, Joanna, the head of marketing for Chambers Gin. The worry was so plain on her face it broke his heart. "We'll turn a corner," Marcus said. "By the time we host the media night at the new distillery, we'll be on our way."

"I don't want you to think I don't trust you or your vision, Marcus. I absolutely do," his father continued. "It's just that the entire family's livelihood is on the line. I don't want to get in so far over our heads that we're all left with nothing. That's not the legacy I hoped to leave behind, and it's definitely not the future I want for my children or my grandchild."

"I'll make it work, Dad. I don't want you to worry about it." *Leave the worrying to me.*

A pregnant pause filled the room. "Okay, son. I trust you. I've got some calls to return, but I'll speak with you and JoJo on Friday, right?"

"Yes. Friday. Speak to you then."

"Bye, Dad." Joanna pressed the end button on the phone in the center of the conference table. "He's so stressed. I don't think I've ever heard him so stressed."

Marcus tapped his pen on the all-too-thin stack of orders for the US gin, Chambers No. 9. "It's not like we can blame him. We aren't even close on our projections." Marcus ran his hand through his hair and turned to stare out the office window overlooking the New York City skyline. And to think he'd been so sure they could capture the imagination of US consumers. They'd come nowhere close. He had the expertise to revive the family business, and he'd dip into his personal financial accounts if needed, but his resources did have their limits. That meant the clock was ticking. Chambers No. 9 needed a big boost, as quickly as possible.

When his father had swallowed his pride and admitted he needed help saving Chambers Gin, Marcus had let his adoration for his father and his deep devotion for his family lead the way. Leaving a highly successful and lucrative job as a European securities trader behind, he'd accepted this new challenge, no questions asked. He'd insisted only that his father trust him on this one point—they had to expand into the massive US market, and that meant launching a new artisan gin. Chambers No. 9. Cocktail culture had become big business, and there was a niche to be filled with carefully crafted spirits. Bold expansion was the only way. Go big or go home, as the Americans loved to say.

"We're just off to a slow start," he said, steeling himself. They would get out of this, and he would lead the way. He wouldn't let anyone down. "Distribution is getting better every day, and we're making inroads. It's just going to take longer than we'd hoped. People don't change their drinking habits overnight."

"They do if there's a reason to. Like a big piece of

media attention or a celebrity endorsement. Something that could go viral."

"The media plan is solid and very aggressive. We just got confirmation that *International Spirits* wants to interview me and put it on the cover. That's big."

Joanna closed her eyes, rested her head on her shoulder and unleashed a snore. "I'm sorry. Did you say something? I was so bored by the thought of *International Spirits* magazine that I fell asleep."

"Hey, that's a big coup, and it's an important player in our industry. Oscar Pruitt is a very influential journalist. Dad's been courting him for years."

"It's not going to set the world on fire. We need to find something for people to get excited about. Really excited. Something unexpected. Something sexy."

Marcus sat back in his chair. Viral videos, memes and celebrities were not at all what he'd envisioned for Chambers No. 9, but he could be onboard with sexy and unexpected. "You're right. Tell you what. We'll do some brainstorming with the rest of the marketing team tomorrow. Perhaps we just need to get a bit more creative."

Marcus's phone lit up with a text. The message was from Ashley, their first interaction since the night before, when she'd grabbed his arm and managed to annoy him with her nonsense about hiding.

Busy? I need to ask you a question.

He tapped out a reply. What is it? The last thing he wanted was Ashley springing a surprise on him, like asking if her contractor could start running saws at five a.m. tomorrow.

An invitation. May I call? Ashley replied.

"Who are you texting?" Joanna asked nonchalantly. At twenty-eight, she might've been three years younger than him, but she could be a mother hen. She'd certainly kept close tabs on him since things went south with his marriage.

"My neighbor. Ms. George. Something about an invitation."

"An invitation? From Ashley George? Have you two patched things up? Whatever it is, you should say yes." Joanna sounded entirely too optimistic for his taste. And pushy. Joanna hadn't even tried to disguise her hope that Marcus would jump into the dating pool with both feet, starting with Ashley. She was, after all, the toast of the entire city, drop-dead gorgeous and, conveniently enough, right across the hall.

Ashley also wasn't a real option. He'd learned that on their date. Their conversation sent up red flag after red flag, culminating with the story of how she and her last boyfriend had broken up because she wasn't ready to have children. That had prompted him to ask for the check and give her nothing more than a handshake at the end of the night. It wasn't like he'd been on the verge of proposing marriage, but he had no business spending time with a woman who didn't share his vision for a relationship. He and Lila were a package deal. No getting around that.

And there was great urgency to his situation. Lila would soon be old enough to remember growing up without a mum. His mother was one of the most important people in his life. He wasn't about to let Lila go without. Watching that would be even worse than seeing Chambers Gin go belly-up. "No patching anything up for me and Ms. George. We're doing our best to tolerate each other." He looked down at his phone again. How he despised texting. Dialing Ashley's number, he shooed Joanna away, but she shook her head, making it clear she was staying.

"Is there a problem, Ms. George?" he asked when she answered.

"No. And please, call me Ashley."

He sat back in his seat, avoiding eye contact with his sister. "What can I do for you?"

Joanna pulled out a pad of paper and wrote furiously. She shoved it across the table and thumped it with her finger. *Be nice!*

"I'm calling with a business proposition."

He'd been bracing for bad news about her apartment project. Business was indeed the last thing he'd expected to be brought up. "Go on."

"Before I say anything, you have to promise me that you won't breathe a word of this to anyone."

Now she really had his curiosity piqued. A secret? "I don't like making promises I'm not certain I can keep."

She huffed on the other end of the line. "You relish any opportunity to be a pain in my side, don't you? Look, I understand you're expanding Chambers Gin in the States. The network is throwing a big party for the premiere of my new season. They'd like to offer you a sponsorship spot that night, at no cost to your company aside from providing your new gin for the guests. Your logo will be everywhere. The guest list is chock-full of celebrities, and they'll all be drinking your gin. The network publicists can work their magic for you."

"Why would you do that for me? And why would I need to keep that a secret?"

She grumbled, "I'm getting to that part. I need you to come to the party. With me. As my date."

For a moment, Marcus wasn't entirely sure of what she'd just said. "I only date women I'm serious about. Because of Lila."

"Then it's perfect, because I don't date at all right now. And I'm not talking about anything more than you taking me to the party and pretending you like me. The network wants me on the arm of a handsome man, I'm not seeing anyone, and you're literally the last man I've been on a date with."

The part of him that warred with her over her apartment wanted to snicker that he was her only option, but the situation also genuinely struck him as a bit sad. "I'm not entirely sure that *Manhattan Matchmaker* and Chambers Gin is the right match. I don't see the correlation between the two brands."

"You want to appeal to young, hip customers? My demographic is all about young and hip."

"And Mrs. White."

"She's a lot hipper than you."

"That's up for debate." He was making her angry, which didn't entirely bother him. Nothing like some good verbal sparring with a beautiful woman to get the blood pumping.

"Well? Will you? Just think of what this could do for your business."

She might have been right about that. He and Jo-anna had been discussing exactly that, and judging by the look on his sister's face, she'd pop off at him if he said no to this. "Yes. I'll do it."

"You will?"

"Yes, I will. Please don't tell me you're angry with me for saying yes."

"No. Not angry. Just surprised, that's all. You fight me on everything."

It's easier to convince myself I'm not so damn drawn to you. "I won't lie. Chambers Gin could use the help. The American market is a big mountain to conquer."

"Okay, then. It's Thursday night. Eight o'clock. I'll have a car for us at seven thirty."

"I'll come round your place at seven-fifteen."

"I'm capable of meeting you at the elevator, you know."

"Ashley, I'm a gentleman. A gentleman always picks a lady up for a date."

Three

Ashley hardly recognized the woman in the mirror. Same face as hers, same hair and nose. Same eyes. But this was the familiar wrapped up in an entirely new and very expensive package. Poised on a pedestal, she twisted from side to side, admiring the sublime lines of the gown designed for her by Peter Richie. *Designed for her.* Since the *Manhattan Matchmaker* ride had started, there had been countless times when she'd wondered whether she was awake or dreaming. Today was just another to add to the list.

Peter shook his head slowly as if he couldn't believe what he was seeing. "Absolutely. Stunning."

He planted both hands at his waist, studying her. A woman with a mouth full of straight pins kneeled at Ashley's feet, adjusting the hem of the gown.

Ashley wrestled with her innate need to deflect attention from herself. "The dress is beautiful. You're absolutely right. Thank you so much for doing this. You have no idea how much I appreciate it." She glanced down, only to catch the woman rolling her eyes. Had she said something stupid? Was it uncool to be thankful? She wasn't entirely sure what she was supposed to say in this situation other than thank you. Her mother had always been emphatic when she was growing up: *"No one will ever fault you for having good manners."*

Peter let out a deep belly laugh. "No, doll. Not the dress. You. You're stunning. All eyes are going to be glued to you at that party."

Ashley swallowed, or at least attempted to. It was hard to get past the lump in her throat. The thought of all eyes glued to her made her exponentially more nervous about the party. Those gatherings were difficult—everyone vying for a piece of her, but it was always a bit superficial. Lots of compliments and praise, but not much in the way of real conversation. No, it was all "keep doing what you're doing" and "we just want more." How much more of this was there? One day the world would tire of the Manhattan Matchmaker. It happened to everyone who ended up in the spotlight as she had, and when it ended, it always seemed to end badly. Tastes changed. Fads came and went. She didn't want to be reduced to that, but someday she would. In some ways, it would be a big relief, but it would mean that her fabulous ride was over.

People assumed that since she was on TV, she'd wanted the limelight. That wasn't the case for her at all. Her confidence in what she was doing and in her ability to do it were unwavering, but it was the other piece of the puzzle that gave her problems. She didn't want her face on the sides of buses. She wanted to match people. She wanted the world to believe in true love. In a world where there was so much bad, she wanted people to remember that there was good.

"I'll be sure to tell everyone that all of the credit for the world's most perfect dress goes to you," Ashley said to Peter.

"Keep talking like that and I'll keep you in party dresses forever." He winked at Ashley then held out his hand to help her step off the pedestal. "You're done, sweetie. The girls will have your dress ready by the end of the day. We'll have it sent to your apartment."

"Oh no. Send it to my office, please. I'm in the middle of a huge apartment project, and it's a total mess."

Ashley left Peter Richie's design studio in the Garment District and opted to walk along 8th Avenue to her building on the Upper West Side. She probably wouldn't make it all the way in heels, but she'd try. It was too beautiful a spring day to not enjoy the splendor of the city. Sporting her biggest Jackie O sunglasses and with her hair tucked up in a hat to avoid being spotted on the street, she set out on her way.

What was left of the afternoon sun peeked between the buildings, the late-April air warming her enough to make her shed her cardigan, draping it over her arm. South Carolina would always be home, but she couldn't see herself living anywhere but New York for the foreseeable future. The city was simply too much fun, brimming with its own kind of beauty. Sure, it could also be a very lonely place, but changing that, one couple at a time, was her charge. There was love to be found in the city that never sleeps. And she was just the girl to give it a push.

After a good twenty blocks, her feet had had all they could take, and she hailed a cab. It didn't take long before they were stuck in rush hour traffic, so she took the chance to call her mom.

"Hello, sugarplum," her mother answered.

As welcome as the sun she'd soaked up along her walk, Vivian George's sugary South Carolina accent was all Ashley needed to shake off the vestiges of her stressful day and feel much more like herself. "Hey, Mama." Her voice cracked simply out of happiness. If she closed her eyes, she could smell her mother's cooking and remember exactly what it was like to grow up in a house where there might have been little money to pay the bills, but love made it seem as if they wanted for nothing.

"You'll be happy to know we're having nearly thirty people over for the premiere of *Manhattan Matchmaker*. I wish we could have you here, honey, but I know you're busy."

It'd been two months since she'd been home, and that'd been only for a few days. It was difficult for her to get away. Work was a constant demand on her time. And that didn't assuage even an ounce of guilt. "I need to come home. And I will. Or maybe you and Daddy could come up to see me. I can book you first-class tickets, and you can stay in my guest room. It'll be so beautiful when the apartment is done. I really want you both to see it."

"I know you do. I really do. We'll have to see how your dad is doing. Travel would take an awful lot out of him."

"I could pay a nurse to travel with you. You wouldn't have to do anything. I swear it wouldn't be much trouble."

"And that's so generous of you, really. But I don't want to make any promises, Ash. He doesn't even like it when we go to the grocery store. New York would be a big undertaking. We'll talk about it."

Ashley saw through the cab window that they were close to arriving at her building. "I just really want you to see it. That's all." She knew deep down that her parents understood her success. Still, she wanted them to see the physical manifestation of it, outside the things she paid for that they saw every day. She wanted to show them that she had done well for herself, and done well for the family.

Four

The antique rocker in Lila's nursery was the perfect place for a daddy-daughter summit. "So, Lila, Daddy's going on a date tonight, but it's very important that you know that you will always be the most important woman in my life."

Lila looked up at him quizzically. "Hi." She palmed the side of his face and smiled, rubbing her tiny fingers over the stubble along his jaw.

He chuckled quietly. *Hi* was her new word, and she was eager to use it. "Hi, yourself."

"Hi," Lila replied.

Joanna, over that night as babysitter, was listening in, leaning against the doorway. She stretched out her arms. "Want me to take her? You really don't want to be holding a baby while wearing a tux, do you? You're begging for a disaster. She'll drool all over you."

Begging for a disaster. Fitting description of what he was all dressed up for. "I'm getting my last few kisses before I have to go to this wretched party."

Sure enough, a droplet of drool fell from the corner of Lila's mouth, dropping down onto his black suit jacket.

"See?" Joanna grabbed a clean washcloth from the top of the nursery bureau. "She's going to ruin your suit." She crouched down next to them, wiping away the moisture that had collected on Lila's lips. "Daddy just needs those teeth to come in so he can get a little more sleep and we can all stop doing so much laundry."

Marcus shrugged. "It doesn't bother me at all. It means she's still a baby. I'm in no hurry for her to grow up." Indeed, he wasn't. He'd take millions more moments exactly like this one. Freeze time and let him stop the clock on the impossible search for the one woman on the planet to take on the role of his wife and Lila's mother.

"I'm glad you're going tonight, Marcus. Really, I am. I hope you are, too."

"Happy for our business. This is nothing but a business arrangement. You know that. Ideally it'll be a productive one. You wanted something out of the ordinary. This is certainly that."

"Actually, I believe I said I wanted something sexy and exciting. It could be that, too."

He'd been bracing for sexy and exciting. He was ill-equipped to deal with either, especially the former.

Joanna stood and took Lila from him. "Now go, before I shoo you out the door. Stay out as late as you want. I certainly don't want you coming home before midnight."

"Why not?"

"Because if you do, it means you haven't had any fun, and Lord knows you could use some fun, Marcus. Loosen that tie at some point. Live a little."

He got up out of the chair, stopping to give Lila one more kiss on her cheek. "Good night, darling. Tell barmy Auntie Jo that I'll be home by midnight."

He strolled out of the apartment and across the hall. He knocked at Ashley's door, not surprised she didn't answer immediately. Muffled strains of popular dance music came from her apartment—another way in which they were polar opposites. He preferred '60s soul.

He tugged at his shirtsleeves and straightened his collar, which felt a bit as if it was choking him. He had to wonder what a woman with a career in reality television would wear to a party thrown in her honor. An ostentatious monstrosity—pink, he guessed—most likely with sequins. Lord help him. He was going to need several drinks tonight. Luckily there'd be plenty of Chambers No. 9 on hand.

He knocked again. The music stopped.

The door flung open. "Don't even say it," Ashley blurted. Her cheeks were flushed. Her eyes flashed in their usual near-manic state. "I'm late. I know it."

Marcus didn't speak. Or blink. Ashley's hair and makeup were done up. The rest of her was…wrapped in a fluffy white bath towel.

"I need two minutes to get dressed. The hair and makeup people just left, and my phone has been ringing like crazy." With a wave, she invited him inside.

Marcus closed the door behind him, his eyes as dry as parchment. He still hadn't blinked. Not once, and it wasn't from shock that Ashley might be late for her own party. It was the damn towel. He hadn't been so close to a beautiful woman in that state of undress in a while, and this wasn't just any woman. This was the woman he'd been trying like hell to stay away from. Every inch of his body felt a prodigious tug as Ashley rushed down the hall, showing slender legs, bare feet and naked shoulders. She left a damning smell of summer rain and vanilla in her wake. The sweet fragrance begged him to follow her. He cleared his throat, feeling as though he needed an oxygen mask. "No worries," he muttered, but she was already gone.

Eager to set his mind straight, he turned away and surveyed the apartment. The layout mirrored Marcus's, but it was otherwise in disarray—tarps draped over furniture, building supplies in every corner of the open space. A patchwork of construction paper blanketed the floor, and an enormous chandelier, cocooned in plastic, hung over the dining room table. How could she live in such bedlam? He wouldn't have lasted five minutes. It would have had him at sixes and sevens—completely crazy—in no time. The room smelled of fresh paint, with the faintest trace of

Ashley's perfume not just shadowing him but needling him. Taunting him. Reminding him that the woman he *wanted* and the woman he *needed* were two entirely separate people.

"I told you it would only take me a minute," Ashley said from behind him.

He turned, ill-prepared for her wardrobe change. No pink monstrosity. Oh no. That would've made things too easy on him. Instead, she wore a silvery gray gown of impeccable taste. Delicate, silky straps skimmed her shoulders. The neckline was sublime, dipping just low enough to please him greatly…and make him wish his pants were a bit roomier. Her golden-blond hair was in an elegant twist to the side. She closed in on him as if she floated on air, quite possibly the breath that had been knocked from his lungs by surprise.

She was grace in motion, not at all what he'd expected. Just like a few nights ago in the hall, when she'd grabbed his arm, he struggled to understand why his libido had formed one opinion of Ashley and his logical mind had formed another.

"What?" she asked, looking down at her dress and turning, again afflicting him with her intoxicating smell. "Is it too much? Too fancy?"

It's perfect. You're perfect. Except that she was otherwise the opposite. He needed to forget the way she made him feel at this moment, and remember the way she'd made him feel every time she did or said something that screamed, "I'm not the right woman."

He shook his head as fog encroached on his thoughts. "No. You look fine."

She arched both eyebrows, making her vibrant brown eyes appear even larger. "At least I don't have to worry about you killing me with kindness."

He had to change the course his mind kept veering onto, one where their business arrangement abruptly ended with a deep kiss and his hands dragging those skinny dress straps off her shoulders. "Remember, tonight is all about business." He gestured to the front door. "Shall we?"

They met the limousine down in the parking garage after Ashley explained that some of her fans had been spotted outside their building. He added that to the list of reasons Ashley was all wrong for him—the intrusion of her public. He didn't like the idea of tallying negatives and essentially building a case against Ashley, but most of the time, the list made it easier to ignore his attraction.

Ashley fidgeted in her seat, repeatedly opening a compact mirror, checking her makeup and sighing.

"Everything alright?" he asked.

"Oh, sure. Just a few butterflies."

He wasn't sure what sort of wildlife had chosen to inhabit his own chest and stomach. He only knew that something was going on in there. He took a deep breath. Tonight was about saving his family's business. Nothing else. Tomorrow he and Ashley would go right back to their semiregular spats over drywall dust and construction noise. That he could manage much better.

"We should probably get our stories straight," Ashley said. "People will want to know how we met. How serious we are."

The notion of constructing a romance struck him as all wrong. That wasn't the way things were supposed to happen, but Ashley was used to it. Her job was orchestrating love, or at least the appearance of it. "Can't we keep it simple and truthful? We met because we're neighbors and we're taking it one day at a time. That's satisfactory, isn't it?"

"What if people ask about our first date? If we're truthful about that, everyone will know we're not a real couple."

Marcus cleared his throat. "Is it any of their business?"

"The press will say it's their business. We'll get skewered if we don't say something." She sat back in her seat, compulsively closing and opening the jeweled clasp of her small silver handbag. "We'll tell people we went to dinner and sparks flew. We'll skip the part about how you shook my hand at the end of the night and essentially started the Wars of the Roses the next day."

The woman had no fear of uncomfortable subjects. "I was being a gentleman that night. I didn't want to lead you on."

"Nor did you allow me to explain myself. I had one too many glasses of wine that night, you know. I was nervous. I say stupid things when I'm nervous."

Flashes of light came through the darkened limousine windows as they pulled up to the curb, thankfully putting an end to that particular strain of conversation. The car stopped and idled. The photographers outside continued taking pictures.

"Just follow my lead with the photographers. I've trained myself to do exactly what they want. It's fairly painless. I promise." She reached over and patted his knee. "And please relax tonight. I know you can be charming. I've seen you do it. That's the Marcus I need at this party, not your normal grumpy self."

His spine stiffened. Why did she continue to use those words? *Grump. Curmudgeon.* She had no idea what he'd been through, the trials that necessitated his serious nature. He wasn't about to launch into an explanation now. "I know how to act at a party. Don't you worry about me."

"Fine. Let's see how you do."

The driver opened the door. The instant Ashley rose from the car, the crowd roared with excitement, fans and photographers shouting her name. She stepped on to the red carpet and turned to him, taking his hand, offering an enchanting smile with plump pink lips that begged for a gentle nip. He was transfixed by that look on her face, so genuine and warm. It made a surreal moment even more so—the object of his mysterious weakness, reaching for him. He had no choice in front of this audience but to go with it. He clutched her impossibly soft fingers and trailed behind her, stepping square into the lion's den.

Cameras were everywhere, all pointed at the two of them. The more persistent the flashes, the tighter Ashley gripped his hand, the closer she pulled him.

She seemed to crave the security of someone by her side, and his instinct told him to protect her, even when he knew it was the wrong inclination, one to fight with everything he had.

She smiled wide as the photographers snapped their pictures, beguiling the masses before them as if she'd been born to do this. *Butterflies, my ass.* Seeing the Manhattan Matchmaker in action, he knew he was being sucked in just as the rest of the world was, but there was only so much he could do about it. He was there to be the handsome man on her arm, and he had to play that role. That meant drinking in the vision of her so the cameras could snap their pictures, even when every second had him further under her spell and it would take a lengthy internal dialogue to wrench himself from it later.

One photographer asked to see the back of Ashley's dress. She let go of Marcus's hand for a moment and turned, flashing a sexy look over her shoulder that nearly left him flat on the red carpet. He was already losing all sense of direction. This was not good. He had four long hours ahead of him of pretending to be her charming, smitten date. He needed a mantra, something he could repeat until it became innate. *Don't fall for her, Marcus. Don't fall for her.*

Five

Ashley had promised herself she'd sweep into this opulent ballroom relaxed, with an easy, confident smile on her face. She'd walk in like she owned the place—crystal chandeliers, expensive champagne and all. Heck, this *was* her party. Tonight was all about her.

Precisely the problem. Confronted with the throng of people in the jam-packed ballroom, she knew how empty the promise had been. She always managed to say the wrong thing or get flustered when someone asked her too many personal questions. She wasn't built for fancy parties and dealing with hundreds of people at one time. Dinner for two, no press or media, was much more her speed.

The masses closed in when they spotted Marcus

and her—a sea of eagerly advancing faces wanting a picture, voices offering greetings and questions, hands reaching out and touching her. Some touching Marcus. The inquisition about him started at a fever pitch.

"Tell us about your date."

"Where'd you find the handsome Brit?"

"How did you keep him a secret?"

"You two look so perfect together. Has the matchmaker made her own match?"

Her pulse picked up. If she was already feeling panicked, wanting to escape, this would be a long night. She scanned the crowd for Grace but saw her nowhere. Ashley had no choice but to smile politely and nod in agreement when someone congratulated her. She laughed nervously at bad jokes. Music thumped loudly. The din of voices became almost paralyzing as people talked over each other.

She and Marcus were pressed tightly against each other under the crush of the crowd. Marcus had handled it all beautifully, being specific enough and deflecting when appropriate, but once the verbal onslaught became truly overwhelming, he cast his magical green eyes down at her. In that moment, she saw comfort in them, not the man who disliked her so greatly.

She popped up onto her tiptoes and spoke into his ear, gripping his strong shoulders, loving the scratch of his five o'clock shadow against her cheek. "I'm a little thirsty. Can we get a drink?"

"Brilliant. I think we both could use one."

She squeezed his hand in response, landing back on her heels. He didn't flinch, as if he could take the pressure however long she chose to strangle his fingers. And she liked that feeling. A lot. It felt as if she could test him and he would never, ever fail. He was precisely what she needed at that moment. A handsome British rock.

Marcus began winding them through the crowd. She walked by every person she didn't really want to talk to and waved, shrugged her shoulders, pointed to Marcus and mouthed, "He wants a drink." So far, he'd been a dream date. Of course, he was her fake date. Not a man who wished to take her anywhere by choice other than an unpleasant apartment board meeting. Not a man who wished to end an evening together with anything more than a cold, detached handshake.

For now, she'd pretend that he really did want to be with her and that she hadn't been so stupid as to say the things she'd said the night they went on their date—the endless ramblings about how her last boyfriend had dumped her because her job was too insane and she wasn't cut out for having kids. She'd never even had the chance to explain to Marcus that James was eleven years older than her and, at the age of forty, on a completely different timetable. Plus, he'd been a jerk of inordinate magnitude when she'd dared to express the tiniest doubt about their future.

So, in the interest of pretending that she and Marcus were a real match, it was time to play the role of

Manhattan Matchmaker, the woman Marcus and everyone else in this room wanted a piece of.

"Gin and tonic?" Marcus asked when they finally reached the bar.

She nodded. "Sounds perfect."

A man tapped Marcus on the shoulder and introduced himself as Alan, one of the network accountants. "I'm on my second drink made with this Chambers No. 9, and I have to say, I'm very impressed."

The bartender slid their drinks across the bar, and Ashley took a gulp.

"Isn't it the most delicious thing you've ever tasted?" she replied, even though this was her first taste. If she and Marcus were going to convince anyone that they were a real pair, she'd be well acquainted with Chambers No. 9 by now. She took a second drink, a sip this time. It truly was lovely—in taste and in the way it took the edge off. By the bottom of the glass, she'd be much better equipped to carry on countless conversations.

"Thank you both," Marcus said, partaking of his drink, continuing his conversation with Alan.

A nonstop parade of people approached Ashley, most asking for tidbits on the upcoming slate of new episodes. "What's the most unlikely pairing you put together this season?" one entertainment reporter asked.

"Probably a pair of lawyers from rival law firms. I've never seen two people argue as much as they did. The production team was sure I'd missed the mark, but I could see the attraction between them. Once they set aside their egos and their issues, they fell hard. It's one of my favorite episodes this year."

Marcus listened and nodded. "She knows when two people should be together."

"And what about you, Mr. Chambers? Tell me about your gin."

Ashley listened as he spoke about his father and grandfather, his impressive lineage, the history behind Chambers Gin. Ashley had nothing like that to brag about, not that it bothered her. She just didn't like the looks of pity she got if anyone asked about her family and she told them the truth—she'd grown up with two brothers, and their parents loved all of them very much. Other than that, there hadn't been two dimes to rub together, and she wasn't even sure how they'd ever survived.

Marcus was quite the opposite, born with an aristocratic silver spoon in his mouth. He worked hard, though. She'd give him that. He didn't seem content to rest on laurels—those that belonged to him or his family. "Gin is my family's passion, and it really is an art. I started my professional life as a securities trader, but I'm so glad to be running the family business and leading the charge with our new brand in the US."

Grace showed up right on the heels of that conversation. Marcus got them another round of drinks from the bar after Ashley made the introductions.

"He's insanely hot," Grace whispered in Ashley's ear.

"Yeah, I got the memo."

"Has it been okay so far tonight?"

Ashley leaned closer so no one could overhear. "It has. It'll be interesting to see what the ride back to our building is like. He won't have to be nice to me anymore at that point." Several network people and more reporters had inched closer to them. "But I'll catch you up about that tomorrow."

Grace fished her phone from her purse and consulted it. "I have to go. Problem with the guest list. I'll catch up with you later." She patted Ashley on the shoulder. "You're doing great. Just keep smiling."

Grace disappeared into the crowd as Marcus brought their drinks.

"Ashley George, I want to know when exactly you got a boyfriend," a woman said from behind them.

Ashley turned, only to come face-to-face with Maryann, editor for the online gossip site that had published the embarrassing pictures of Ashley buying ice cream on a Saturday night. Maryann was a near-perfect human specimen, long legs and a button nose, but her personality was of the rodent variety.

Ashley cupped her hand around Marcus's ear. "Careful with this one. She's mean."

Marcus offered his hand. "Marcus Chambers. Pleased to meet you. You are?"

"Maryann Powell. *Celebrity Chitchat*. We're the premier gossip website on the East Coast."

Marcus nodded in his distinguished English manner. "Ah. I haven't yet had the opportunity to see your website, but I'm sure it's of the highest caliber."

Ashley snickered and took another gulp of her drink.

"I keep close tabs on you, Ashley." Maryann pointed right at her. "It's my job to know if you have a boyfriend. There's no way this got past me."

Ashley fought the urge to roll her eyes. People like Maryann were exactly the reason she sometimes hated the business of being a so-called celebrity. "We're neighbors, Maryann. That's how we met, and that's how we kept it quiet."

"Right across the hall from each other, as fate would have it," Marcus added.

Marcus had spoken so quickly that it was as if he was finishing her sentence. It came across as perfectly natural and seamless, nothing at all like the true nature of their relationship.

"And?" Maryann asked. "I want juicy details. This is your chance, you know. I could plaster you two all over our home page tomorrow morning. Our site is insanely good for business."

Just then, a photographer popped up behind Maryann and snapped some pictures. The network had granted several news outlets unlimited access to the party. Including Maryann's trashy website, apparently.

"It's quite simple." Marcus put his arm around Ashley. "We went on a date and sparks flew."

Ashley would've beamed at the fact that he'd remembered he was supposed to mention sparks if she wasn't so dumbstruck by having his solid arm draped across her shoulder. He tugged her closer, the way a real boyfriend would. He was even rubbing her upper arm with his fingertips in gentle, swirling circles. She had to make a conscious decision to remain standing. Either the gin was getting to her or that soft brush of his skin on hers was making her light-headed.

"I just think it's weird that I haven't seen you two out anywhere together. This isn't some sort of publicity stunt, is it? We got a zillion comments on those pictures of you buying ice cream, and that wasn't that long ago. The timing seems a little convenient. I know Grace. She's a brilliant publicist. There's no way she was going to let those pictures go unanswered."

If Ashley could've chosen a superpower at that moment, it would've been the ability to make Maryann invisible. As in gone. They needed to get away from her, if only for her own sanity. She put her arm around Marcus's waist and rested her head against his shoulder. She also kicked the side of his shoe as slyly as possible. "Sorry. No big conspiracy." *Just a little one.*

Marcus cleared his throat and cast his sights at Ashley. Judging by the look in his eyes, he'd caught Ashley's drift. "Shall we mingle a bit, love? I'm sure you have an awful lot of people you need to speak with tonight." Marcus turned away, but Maryann grabbed Ashley's arm.

"And a British gin magnate who's a calendar model?" Maryann asked. "A little heavy-handed, don't you think?"

Marcus spun around and confronted Maryann head-on. "I'm sorry, but that calendar is for charity, and there's nearly twenty years of tradition behind it. And my occupation is what it is. My family has been making gin for well over a century. As for the rest of the things you're insinuating, this is Ashley's big night, and I believe it's time for us to, uh…" He scanned the room. "It's time for us to have our first dance."

He grabbed Ashley's hand and barreled through the crowd with her in his wake. They arrived on the dance floor in little time. He settled one hand in hers, placed the other on her waist and steered them toward the center, away from Maryann. "I'm sorry, but we had to get away from that dreadful woman. You do know how to dance, don't you?"

"Of course I do." As a little girl, Ashley had spent many sweltering summer evenings out on the wrap-around porch, listening to music with her parents, learning to dance like a lady. The music tonight wasn't quite the same, taking a decidedly slower—and, to Ashley's chagrin, a much more romantic—turn.

"I don't want to be old-fashioned," Marcus said, "but it is generally considered the man's job to lead."

Ashley wasn't good at this part. Even at the age of seven, she'd been accused of trying to lead. "After all of that with Maryann, you're going to give me a hard time about leading?"

He yanked her tightly against him, sending a surprising shock through her entire body. "Just relax."

"Hey. That's my line." She took a deep breath, far too aware that she was pressed against his rock-hard, heavenly torso. A few layers of clothing gone and this dance would take on a whole new meaning. He wound them through the other couples dancing. He did it so well that they were garnering attention. People were starting to watch them. Once again, under the microscope.

"I'm sorry if what I said was embarrassing for you," he started. "I couldn't stand another word out of that horrible woman's mouth."

Ashley looked up at him, his expression as stern as any other day. Still, for the first time ever, it felt almost as if they were on the same side. "I'm sure she'll make me pay for it eventually, but I'm glad you did it. She had it coming."

"I should probably explain that bit about the calendar. It's silly, really."

"I already know about it. I saw it online."

He smirked. "So you went looking for dirt on me."

"A girl has to be careful. There are a lot of creeps in this city. I had to make sure you hadn't left England to escape a murder charge."

A smile crossed his lips and he shook his head. "Escaping that calendar was a good enough reason on its own to leave England. My sister talked me into it, but I think her motives went beyond charity. I'd only been divorced a few months, and she had this crazy idea it would help me find a woman."

She really wanted to ask him about his ex-wife, but she didn't dare risk upsetting him. She didn't want to leave the security of his arms. "Sounds like your sister could be gunning for my job."

He laughed, which she loved. She'd made him angry so many times. This was a nice change.

"You don't really enjoy all of this, do you?" he asked. "Being the center of attention."

Her normal inclination would be to deny the suggestion, especially coming from him. "You know, I get that this is just part of the job, but I get overwhelmed. My first inclination when I walk into any party is to turn around and run."

"So you do better one-on-one."

Was that flirtation she heard in this voice? No matter his intention, his words made her knees wobble. "I definitely prefer being the center of one person's attention."

"Like now."

"Exactly like now."

The song changed, but Marcus kept her close as if he had no intention of letting go. "People are staring at us, you know."

What was it about his voice that made her so weak in the knees? "I noticed."

"I wonder what they're all thinking."

She swallowed hard but couldn't stop the words coming next. "They're all wondering if we're in love."

"Ah, right. Love." He shook his head. "Your public will become that much more fascinated by you if they think the matchmaker is in love."

"So I'm told."

"And you believe all of that business about there being a true love for everyone? Or is it just for the show?"

Funny, but no one else had ever asked her that question. "I do believe it."

Marcus took a look around the dance floor. All eyes were indeed trained on them. "I'm tempted to give them a show, you know. If nothing else, we could shut up that horrible Maryann woman."

Again, his rich, buttery accent was working its way into her. He could have read her the side of a cereal box and she would've been mesmerized. "What did you have in mind?"

"If we do it, I think we start slowly, give them a taste of what's to come."

Her mind raced at the mention of "do it," especially since she was reasonably certain he didn't mean "it." She had to stay focused if she was going to remain composed. "Of course. We wouldn't want to go too fast." Except that she was thinking about nothing but going very fast, away from this party, away with him.

"I could start by kissing your cheek, whispering in your ear that you look beautiful tonight." He did exactly that as he said it, his warm lips on her face, his hot breath against her ear, skimming the slope of her neck.

Her head was swimming, but a compulsion rose up in her, a need to use this as an excuse to push boundaries just as he had. She reached up and dug her hand into the thick hair at his nape, grazed his ear with her thumb. That one brush of skin on skin was enough to send her into blissful oblivion especially when his mouth parted ever so slightly. "Beautiful, huh? You told me I looked fine."

His eyes were intense, darkening as he focused on her in the soft light of the ballroom. All sound receded. Movement around them slowed. "I lied. You look spectacular."

Heat bloomed in her cheeks. "And you might be the most handsome man I've ever seen. Damn you."

He cupped the side of her face, looking at her as if he'd been planning this all along. There was no hesitation in his eyes, just sheer will and determination. Her heart thumped wildly. His gaze stripped away every defense she had. It felt as if she was stark naked on that dance floor. His face drew closer. His eyes drifted shut. She followed suit. Before she could take a breath, he claimed his kiss.

A frantic flutter started in her chest. The sensation of his giving lips on hers, the wonder of his warmth, spread to her stomach, blanketed her shoulders and legs, heated her cheeks. She rose to her tiptoes and arched into him. *Finally. A kiss.* His approach was commanding and entirely self-assured, his grasp on her so firm. She wasn't sure she'd ever been kissed so masterfully. Then came his tongue, soft and sensual. Gentle. Dizzying.

When they came up for air, her head was in the clouds. Flashes of light surrounded them. So this was what it was like to see fireworks. She'd never been kissed like that. No other man had been in the same league of Marcus's intensity—not even James, who'd been a damn good kisser.

"I hope we gave them what they wanted," he whispered, his eyelids heavy.

She nodded, not knowing what to say, hypnotized by the vision of his lips, wondering what her mouth had to do to invite his to be all over her—her neck, her chest, her everything. If she felt naked and he had the nerve to kiss her, he might as well do it for real. She turned, squinting. Photographers. Cameras. A barrage of flashing lights.

"Because I know I got what I wanted," he muttered.

Six

"We should go." Ashley gazed up at Marcus, his physical presence making it damn near impossible to think. So instead, she relied on what her body told her to do. Her only honest desire at that moment was to be alone with him. Either he'd act as if the kiss had been a mistake, in which case she definitely didn't want anyone within earshot. Or he'd want more. In that case, she wanted a clear, horizontal landing spot. She might never catch him in this mood again.

"You don't have to stay?" he asked.

She shook her head. She knew she'd catch flack for leaving early, but she didn't care—he'd rendered her unable to think through the ramifications of anything. "No. I don't want to answer questions about the kiss. It's my party and I've had enough." Her arm hooked in his, punctuating her declaration.

"Right, then."

They made their exit, Ashley feeling as antsy as she'd felt in a long time, but also loving the feeling of stealing away with Marcus. As guest of honor, Ashley had earned the right to have her limo waiting outside the hotel. They were whisked away into the New York City night, where true dark did not exist—too many lights, too much commotion.

Sitting this close to him, the tingle of his lips still on hers, it was all she could do to remain a lady and wait for a sign, some indication of what he was thinking. Her breaths were shallow as if she couldn't get enough oxygen no matter how much of it she sucked in. She glanced over at him, and he acknowledged her with half a smile.

"Some night, huh?" he asked.

She scoured her brain for something impossibly sexy to say but couldn't come up with much. "It ended better than I thought it would."

He laughed quietly, but she wasn't in the mood for him taking her answer as comedy. Silently but deliberately, she planted her left hand on the seat between them, palm up, asking for his touch without a single word. She wanted him to look at her, but his sights were set on her hand. Was this the right thing to do? It felt as if it was, but maybe that was the influence of his kiss. Her heart, having no clue as to how he'd respond, chose to canter with all the grace of a newborn filly.

After several agonizing moments, he reached for her hand, but he didn't actually take it. Instead, his fingers caressed the cup of her palm, back and forth.

"This is the life line," he said, tracing the one that started near her thumb and curved down to the heel of her hand.

Her normally restless self was as enthralled as could be by his touch, which sent excitement bubbling up inside her. She turned to him. Wherever any of this led, she wanted it, but they had blocks to go until they'd be back to their building. The thought of waiting was an excruciating one, but she also knew better than to start things in the limousine. *Keep your clothes on, Ash.*

"If I remember correctly, yours says that you're someone people count on in difficult times," he said.

She liked that. She wanted people to be able to rely on her, especially her parents, even when she felt as though she couldn't keep her own life together. But were these words really coming out of Marcus's mouth? "You know palm reading?"

"It's called palmistry, and it's been popular in the UK for ages. My great-great-grandmother was a member of the Chirological Society of Great Britain." His brow furrowed with feigned seriousness. "They were very concerned with preserving the art of palmistry and keeping charlatans from abusing it."

"This is literally the last thing I ever expected from you, Marcus Chambers."

He smiled, his eyes connecting with hers, expos-

ing her vulnerabilities. "Maybe you aren't as perceptive as you think you are."

"I'm incredibly perceptive, and I perceive that
you're just very good at keeping things to yourself."

He looked down again and softly traced another
line on her hand. "This is the head line. Yours says
that you pick up on other people's feelings. You sym-
pathize with them."

"See? Perceptive. I told you so."

"It also means that you change your mind a lot.
I'm not sure that's the best quality. It can make things
difficult for the people in your life."

"It depends on how you see it. Some people might
say that means I'm flexible."

"Your heart line is split in two." He shifted to the
deep crease closest to her fingers.

"So you can tell that my heart has been broken
before?" Her breaths came quicker. Could he see
that she was hurting? That she was lonely? That she
needed love?

"Actually, that means you have a habit of putting
other people's feelings first. You should concentrate
on what you want, Ash."

That was the first time he'd called her by her nick-
name, and God, she loved the familiarity of it. He de-
viated from the lines and swirled gentle circles in her
palm. She sucked in a breath. *He's killing me.* How
a man could command anything he wanted with the
simple brush of his fingers was beyond her. She knew
only that Marcus could.

"Your skin is so soft," he muttered with a sexy

undertone of gravel in his voice. "I could touch it forever."

"I could let you forever." That was the truth. It felt so perfect.

He shifted in his seat and his jacket fell open— just enough for her to see that he was as turned on by this situation as she was. For the first moment of the entire night, she felt as though she could relax. No man changed his mind in that particular state. Or at least, not that she'd ever experienced.

Mercifully, the car turned in to the parking garage of their building. It was if she'd been wrenched from a fabulous dream, only to wake up and realize that real life was even better. She cleared her throat, smoothed her hair, thanked the driver. She hadn't scrambled out of a car so fast in her entire life. They hurried inside. She was so relieved the elevator was empty.

Now that things were going the way she'd hoped, she wanted it to be perfect. "Did you, um, want to come over to my place?" she asked.

"I thought you'd never ask," he replied, taking her hand, looking at her with a smile that said he wanted to consume her. She was more than ready to be breakfast, lunch and dinner.

"Do you need to check in with the babysitter or something?"

"My sister is watching Lila. She's fine."

The elevator dinged and she took his hand, rushing to her door. Once inside, she dropped her handbag on the foyer table, and he very quickly removed his jacket and left it there, as well.

She took his hand and placed it on her shoulder, using his thumb to push off the strap, eager for more than his suit coat to end up on the table.

"Well, then," he said, smirking, wrapping his arm around her waist and coaxing the second strap off with his other hand.

"You told me in the limo to concentrate on what I want. I'm following orders." The light of the city filtered in through the windows behind him, outlining his broad frame, casting shadows on his strong jaw and down the contours of his neck.

"You are so beautiful," he said, caressing her cheek. "I can't wait to see the rest of you."

"Me, too. I want to find out if that calendar was false advertising or if you really do look that good without a shirt."

He laughed. "So you really did look?"

"Yes, Marcus. I did."

Ashley popped up onto her tiptoes and raised her arms up onto his shoulders. She kissed him with surprising force. He loved that about her—it was like kissing a firecracker dressed up in dynamite. She was a bundle of pure excitement and enthusiasm. She reminded him that he was alive. He couldn't have stopped drinking in her life force if he'd wanted to. He'd asked himself in the limo if this was a good idea, but he was tired of that question. She wanted him. He wanted her. They were two grown people, capable of making their own decisions. Thinking was for later.

Their lips mashed together eagerly, tongues wound

around each other in an endless spiral. He held her flat against him, letting her feel exactly how hard he was, how much he wanted her. He reached for the zipper at the back of her dress and dragged it down. Her breath caught as his hand explored her silky back, his fingers drawing up and down her spine, dipping lower on each pass until he reached the lacy fabric of what felt like incredibly skimpy panties. He had to see for himself what that was all about.

"Can we go into your bedroom?" he asked, nearly breathless.

"Yes." She grabbed his hand, holding up her dress with the other, and leading him down the hall she'd traipsed through in a towel at the beginning of their night. *The towel.* Could he convince her a shower was in order at some point? His mind churned with possibilities—all of the things he wanted to do to her, the things he wanted her to do to him.

They arrived at her room, and although it was difficult to see much in the dim light, there was a massive bed and that was enough.

She turned to him and let the dress fall to the floor. His eyes couldn't take in the landscape of her beautiful body fast enough. Her slender legs. The generous curve of her hips. Her gorgeous, pert—and naked—breasts.

"No bra?" He cupped her velvety skin gently with his hands, watching her reaction as he dragged his thumbs across her nipples, the skin tightening beneath his touch. Everything below his waist responded in kind.

"Not in that dress, no. I don't really need it." She moaned quietly as he continued to roam with his hands, caressing her velvety skin. "We need to get you out of these clothes."

He'd been so lost in the wonder of her naked body that he hadn't even realized he was still mostly dressed. He yanked off his tie and unbuttoned his shirt, watching as Ashley's nimble fingers unlatched his belt and she dropped his pants to the floor. Now all there was between them was her panties, his boxers and the willingness to set aside disagreements for a much more enjoyable neighborly meeting.

He watched as she flattened her hands against his chest and began moving down his torso with delicate kisses, but the clock on the bedside table caught his eye. He'd promised he would be home before midnight, and the time had nearly arrived. Joanna had told him to stay out, but guilt began to eat at him.

Ashley climbed onto the bed and curled a finger with a sly grin on her face. "Get over here, Chambers."

Her spark was enough to make him do hundreds of things he'd told himself he wouldn't do. He stretched out next to her, and his hands roved over her smooth stomach. He leaned down and pressed a kiss to her breast, then sucked her nipple softly. Ashley arched her back and practically purred. "That feels so good," she muttered, as if that "so" had fifty *o*'s. He flicked his tongue while he inched his hand to the waistband of those tiny panties and began tugging them past her hips.

Ashley lifted her bottom off the bed. "Touch me, Marcus. Please. I'm dying." She squirmed beneath his touch as he slipped his fingers between her legs and found her warm apex. "Yes. There."

She rolled toward him and kissed him recklessly as he caressed that tight bundle of nerves. He sensed the tension in her body quickly, punctuated by short, raspy breaths. He'd forgotten what it was like to have a woman at his mercy, to be able to give her pleasure that made it feel as though he was invincible. "Is that what you like, Ash? Is that how you like it?"

"Yes," she nearly growled. "And talk to me, Marcus. I like a man who talks to me in bed."

It was not a request. It was a demand, and it made him that much more determined to make her come like she never had before. He lightened his touch—teasing, toying. "I'll talk as long as you play along."

"Is everything a negotiation with you?" She shifted, resting her upper thigh between his legs, creating sublime friction between them. "Because I'd be willing to concede a lot right now."

Her quick wit only turned him on more. He had to focus on her pleasure or he'd go sailing off the cliff in no time. "No bargaining. Just tell me what you want."

"Circles. With your hand. And don't be gentle."

Her words made everything in his body tighten, and he obliged her, upping the pressure, moving in steady rotations with his fingers.

She tilted her head back, pulling away from his kiss while pressing her pelvis hard into his hand. "Yes. Just like that," she gasped. Every breath she took ended in a whimper, growing louder, stronger, more insistent. Then she arched her back and froze, calling out, grabbing his hand and insistently stilling it against her body.

As soon as she caught her breath, she sought his lips, kissing him deeply. She pushed him to his back and climbed on top of him, straddling his hips. It was a good thing he still had his boxers on. This much touching was too much to take. "Tell me you have a condom," she said.

"You don't?"

"I don't. I was taking a break from men, remember? I told you that on our first date."

"I assumed that was a metaphorical break. Not a real one."

She shook her head and kissed him again. "Oh, trust me. It was a real break. I haven't been with another man in months. So please tell me you have a condom or else one of us is going to have to run to the drug store on the corner and buy some."

"No. I have some…" His voice trailed off. He had indeed purchased a box after they arrived in New York, after Joanna had given him the speech about taking chances and opening his heart. "It's just that they're across the hall." Across the hall. Just like his entire life was across the hall. His conscience told him that's where he belonged at that moment, not having sex with a woman he knew wasn't the one.

Stop it. He forced himself to take a deep breath. He had to collect his thoughts. He had a gorgeous woman in his arms, one he'd wanted for months. A deeply passionate woman who was making him feel like the man he used to be. Except the man he used to be had made a lot of mistakes. That man had gone through five years with blinders on, ignoring what was wrong in his failing marriage and forging ahead, pushing, trying to will what he wanted into being.

Was he doing that again? Convincing himself that making love to Ashley would be okay simply because he wanted to? That was such a selfish attitude, it nearly made him sick. He'd sworn he'd never be like that again.

"I can't do this," he said, disbelieving the words as they came from his mouth. He wanted her so badly he could taste it, taste her, as sweetness on his lips. An unforgettable sweetness. And then there was the tide that had engulfed the lower half of his body. How would he just ignore that? It didn't matter. He had to.

Ashley looked down at him with those eyes—sincere and genuine. "I don't understand."

"We both know where this is going, and I can't do that. I can't have a casual affair. Not as a dad. Not with Lila in my life. This is about much more than me."

"I wasn't aware we were having an affair." She rolled off him and grabbed the covers, clutching them to her chest.

He shook his head. "I can't just sleep with you one time. What kind of man would that make me?"

"Who said anything about just sleeping together one time? Why can't we take it slow? Four hours ago I was pretty sure you still hated me. At least give me a chance to catch up. You aren't the only one coming off a bad breakup."

Everything she'd just said was precisely why this wouldn't work. She didn't get it. "I wouldn't characterize my failed marriage as a bad breakup." It had been far worse than that. His failed marriage had nearly destroyed him and it remained to be seen what lasting effects it would have on Lila. He grabbed his trousers from the floor and put them on in a hurry, trying to ignore his physical agony. "There is no siow for me, Ashley. There's more at stake here than a tryst. You're a smart, beautiful, successful woman, and somewhere out there is the perfect man for you. I'm just not him." He pushed his arms through his sleeves, only bothering with a few of the buttons on his shirt.

"But we're still getting to know each other. I like you, in spite of the way you act sometimes. And I think you like me, but you're making a lot of assumptions about what's a good idea and what you think I want."

"I didn't pull these ideas out of thin air. You told me during our first date that your last boyfriend left because you were unwilling to get married and become a mom. I realize that's serious stuff to talk about in the early days, but that's the reality of my situation. There's no getting around it."

"You didn't even let me tell you the whole story that night. I would get married if it was the right situation, but let's not forget that you've spent much of the last several months acting as though you don't even like me."

Marcus knew his behavior hadn't been the best, but he'd never done anything that wasn't completely justified. "And it's clear that the situation between us isn't right. We're attracted to each other, but we're otherwise opposites. I'm serious. You're not."

"Serious? My whole life has been about serious."

"Really? A television show about matchmaking, intermingled with shopping for apartment furniture and dismissing the horrible behavior of your contractor? We have very different ideas of what *serious* means." Even in the dim light of the room, it was clear how badly his words had hurt her. He didn't like hurting a woman, but maybe it was for the best. It would make it easier to stay away from her.

Wrapping herself in the sheets, she hopped off the bed. "Fine. You know what? You're right. We're wrong for each other. Just go."

"Good. Then we agree."

"For once we agree."

Seven

Ashley dropped her purse on her desk, confronted by the black-and-white evidence of Marcus's apparent weak moment last night. The first of many weak moments.

Nearly a dozen daily tabloids had been laid out for her. The kiss graced every cover, with clever headlines like The Kiss Heard Round the World. If only the papers knew the real story. British Hunk Rejects Dateless Matchmaker. Her stomach soured. She should be remembering the kiss fondly, reminiscing about the surprise and newness of that moment—the instant when she'd dared to think Marcus didn't think she was ridiculous.

She plopped down in her chair and began to read the papers. They not only recounted the kiss but also very unsubtly mentioned that she and Marcus had left the party early, right after things got hot and heavy on the dance floor. *Great. Now the whole world is imagining what we didn't actually do last night.*

It was barely past nine a.m. and exhaustion threatened to overtake her, but she didn't dare close her eyes. She'd learned her lesson last night after he'd left her in a state of shock, alone with the memory of what they'd done in her bed. Every sexy moment between them was so surreal now, the unlikeliest events imaginable considering their ill-fated first date and the countless complaints about her apartment that had preceded them.

Seeing a picture of the way it all started last night didn't make it more real, not even when she dragged her finger along the photograph, admiring the way he towered over her, the way she fit so perfectly in his arms. If anything, it made it feel even more like a dream, and one with a very sad ending. Had Marcus, the upper-crust Brit, really kissed the girl from a one-gas-station town in South Carolina? Or had he played along with the ruse of a romance with the Manhattan Matchmaker for the benefit of himself and his company? Only to put an end to it when he realized they'd gone much further than he'd ever intended?

She'd seen so many different sides of Marcus last night, it was hard to keep up. There was no longer any doubt in her mind that a fiery, passionate Marcus was beneath his rigid exterior, but he'd built a damn fortress around himself. Had it been a necessity after his divorce? It was the most logical guess, but she didn't have much faith in rational thought, or at least not her own. Logic said that a man with an impressive erection who had an eager and naked woman in his arms didn't hesitate to make love to her. Either she was truly distasteful or something much bigger was keeping him from her. She'd gotten too close to him last night, and as a result, he'd banished her to the other side of the moat, pulled up the drawbridge, and retreated to his own bed.

"Knock, knock." Grace poked her head into Ashley's office. "What a night, huh? Or should I say, what a kiss?" Her eyebrows bobbed up and down.

Ashley should've known she'd get teased about this. "Please don't give me a hard time about it. You asked for romance. We gave it to you." *Romance. Ha. More like no-mance.*

"I would never give you a hard time about this. Are you kidding me? The network brass love you today more than they've ever loved you, which is saying a lot. The ratings for the first episode tonight are going to be massive. Through the roof. They can't wait to see the numbers on Monday so they can start raking in advertisers' cash. There's a whole pile of money to be made, you know."

Money. That was the sole silver lining. Everything else about this made her queasy. Marcus abhorred the idea of her, at least when it came to romance, and the world thought quite the contrary. She was going to get questions about Marcus for days. Weeks, maybe. She knew the tabloids well enough by now. This morning's papers would not be the last of the kiss that blew up in her face.

"I'm happy they're happy. I hope it will help Marcus's business and he'll let me finish my renovations in peace." Her voice trailed off as her eyes were again drawn to a photo of the kiss. Good God, he was sexy. Just looking at the picture made his sexiness resonate in her body, followed by a flood of rejection, sadness and even anger—feelings that did not play well together.

"Hold on a second. Was there not a major love connection last night? Because it sure as hell looked like it."

"Let's just say the connection fizzled." Her voice wobbled, betraying her intention to not let anyone know how much this bothered her.

Grace sat forward. "Are you okay? Do you want to tell me what happened?"

Ashley shook her head. "I really don't want to rehash it. I'm glad that last night was good for business, but it's going to take me some serious time to heal from it. Being rejected by Marcus Chambers is not fun."

"He rejected you?"

"Is that so hard to believe? You know how he feels about me. Last night was just the final nail in the coffin. At this point, all I want is to finish my apartment and avoid him until the day he moves back to England."

"And when is that?"

She cleared her throat. "I think he has a five-year work visa."

"Ashley, this is silly. I'm sure that whatever happened last night was a misunderstanding."

"No way. This is a dead subject. Time to get whatever mileage we can out of last night and move on."

"Uh, yeah, about that. The higher-ups were emphatic with me this morning. They want more of you and Marcus. They want more of this." She leaned forward and tapped one of the newspapers.

Ashley knew she'd heard Grace correctly. She just wasn't happy about it. She and Marcus had to stay away from each other. Better to leave grumpy dogs lie, especially ones who had no qualms about turning down a woman after she'd taken off her designer gown. "You're just going to have to tell them no. Marcus hates me."

"There's no way we'll get the network to buy that. That kiss was convincing." Grace pointed at Ashley's desk. "Look at you two. I'd do anything for a man to kiss me like that, especially if I knew he looked like he does under that suit."

"What is it with you and his abs?" Ashley couldn't stand to look at the photos anymore. It hurt too much. She collected the stack of papers, got up from her chair and plopped them down in Grace's lap. "Marcus Chambers and I are done. Kaput. End of story."

"I didn't want to have to tell you this, but the network is not happy you left the party early. If the papers hadn't come out this morning, you could've been in serious hot water."

"Oh please. I just…" *I just wanted to be alone with him.* "I had a headache."

"Liar. I saw the look on your face when you two walked off the dance floor." Grace sat back in her chair. "What if I told you my job is hanging in the balance?"

"They can't fire you over this. I won't let them."

"I'm talking about a promotion. They're considering me for head of network publicity. Becky Jensen is leaving at the beginning of June."

"Head of the department? For the whole network?"

Grace nodded. "The whole shebang."

Grace had come from similarly humble beginnings, and they always had each other's back. She lived in a postage stamp of an apartment with her sister and had student debt up to her eyeballs. A promotion like that would be a boon for Grace, and well-deserved. She worked as hard as Ashley, maybe even harder.

The guilt wasn't merely crushing, it was suffocating. Ashley couldn't take money out of someone else's mouth, let alone the mouth of a good friend. "I don't know how I can convince him to say yes."

Grace crossed her legs, pulling on her long auburn locks, seeming deep in thought. "You both have to eat, don't you? Just go out to dinner with the man. Remind him how much good it'll do for Chambers Gin."

Ashley sighed, slumping back in her chair. "One dinner?" Why did the task seem so Herculean? Oh, right. Because Marcus had made it clear last night. He couldn't be around her.

"After that, it's your call. We'll just let all the world wonder what you two are doing up in that lovely high-rise apartment building. You do live across the hall from each other, after all. The proximity is nothing but sheer temptation."

Given Ashley's current level of sexual frustration, she couldn't argue, even though she was certain Marcus didn't see it that way at all. "Fine. I'll ask him. But I'm not promising anything."

Grace stood up and clutched the stack of newspapers to her chest, smiling wide, victorious. "Where are you watching the premiere tonight? Do you want to come over?"

Ashley shook her head. "Are you kidding me? The last thing I want to do is watch myself on television."

Marcus couldn't stand to look at the newspapers. Except that he couldn't stand *not* to look at them, either. He'd removed all copies from his personal office, save one tucked away in the bottom-right desk drawer. There'd been more than one moment during the day when he had to see it. See her. See them. Last night had really happened. He'd kissed Ashley. He'd touched her. He'd kissed her and touched her and the entire world had shifted, exactly as he'd feared.

Marcus stepped into Joanna's office just as she hung up the phone. He had to catch up with her. They'd both been working nonstop all day. He nearly collapsed in the chair opposite her desk. The ripple effect of kissing Ashley was rife with bizarre good fortune. New orders and inquiries had left everyone in the office scrambling to keep up.

"That was Dad," Joanna said. "He's right chuffed, Marcus. I haven't heard him so excited in I don't know how long."

He'd had rumblings of this, but only Joanna had spoken directly to their father. It seemed that the kiss heard round the world had taken no time reaching across the pond. "More orders?"

"They've gone through the roof. And it's not just for No. 9. Orders for the original are more than triple what they were for April of last year. All from one day. We're bumping up UK production, and I think we need to take a long, hard look at doing the same in the US."

He would indeed need to speak to their production manager about bringing the new distillery up to peak production. It was a scary proposition, seeing as it hadn't been tested at full capacity.

"Dad asked whether there will be any signage linking Chambers and *Manhattan Matchmaker*. I guess several of the distributors are wondering about it."

Bloody hell. A vision of a cardboard cutout of Ashley holding a bottle of Chambers gin materialized in his head. He could see Joanna wanting to put one out in the reception area. As if it wasn't difficult enough to live across the hall from Ashley, he'd have to walk past that every day. Plus, that was not the image of Chambers Gin his family had worked at cultivating for more than a century. He and Joanna had been working their fingers to the bone to make the US ven-

ture a success, but even a big break like the publicity
of last night needed to be contained. This would get
out of hand in little time if he didn't put a stop to it.
"There's not going to be any signage. Last night was
a one-time thing, and that was that. There is no link
between us and her show."

A cheeky smile crossed Joanna's face. She held up
one of that morning's newspapers. "We could always
just laminate this. From the look of this photograph,
I'd say that Chambers gin and *Manhattan Matchmaker*
are about as linked as can be."

A familiarly unsettling mix of embarrassment and
excitement returned. "That kiss was for the cameras.
And that's all it was. It will not be happening again."
Except that the cameras were a convenient excuse.
Something else was behind it, and he knew it. Something else was behind kissing her in her apartment,
taking off her dress. If he thought about the look on
her face as he'd sent her into oblivion, he felt drunk.
If he thought about what had happened afterward—
his sheer panic—he felt hungover. There was no getting around it. He absolutely had to stay away from
Ashley. He simply wasn't his normal, sensible self
around her.

"Let's not get ahead of ourselves. Last night was
huge for us. And hey, at least you kissed someone."
She giggled, her eyebrows bouncing.

"Please, Joanna. I beg you. I'm a grown man.
Can we stop talking like a bunch of teenagers?" He
brushed away a piece of lint on his pants. "Last night
was a one-time thing and that's it. End of discussion."

Joanna twisted her lips. "Uh, yeah. About that…"

"What?"

"Dad really wants you to take out Ashley again."

"He said that?" Marcus bolted forward in his seat. "He explicitly said that?"

She nodded. "And I have to agree with him. You should at least take her out for a nice meal to thank her for last night. It's great for business and don't forget that it was your idea to expand into the US." Joanna tapped away on her laptop. "I think the fact that you met Ashley and had the chance to take her out is wonderful. You can't argue it's not the best thing that's happened to us since we came to New York." She patted the stack of new orders and wholesale inquiries sitting on her desk. "If you play your cards right, it could be the best thing that's happened in your personal life."

"What is that supposed to mean?"

Joanna closed her laptop and folded her arms across it. "She's lovely, Marcus. And granted, I haven't met her or anything, but she seems like quite a nice woman."

"I know where you're going with this, and you can stop right now. You know my situation, Jo. Better than anyone."

She rose from her seat and rounded to the front of her desk. "What is your situation, Marcus? Working impossible hours to measure up to some imagined standard you set for yourself, then going home and reading a book to Lila? Spending the weekends taking her to the park, but not interacting with another soul in this enormous city? There are thousands of single women in Manhattan, Marcus. Tens of thousands. One of them could make a wonderful wife and mother, but you'll never find her if you don't look."

He crossed his arms in front of him. "I've looked. I've dated three women in the six months since we've been here. That seems like a respectable number to me."

"Including Ashley. And none of them went beyond the first date."

"None of them was right. There's no point in wasting my time with a woman when I know she isn't right." It made perfect sense to him, but he and Joanna had argued about this before. "And you know that dating is a complicated situation for me. I refuse to introduce any of them to Lila until I'm serious. And let's be honest—most women do not want a baby right off the bat."

His heart ached as the words came out of his mouth. Dear, sweet Lila was the most precious thing in the world to him. He still couldn't fathom how Elle had walked out on her, except that he'd witnessed it—the desperate look in Elle's eyes that told him she was equally horrified by her own distaste of motherhood. She didn't want to be a mom, never had, and Marcus had talked her into it. With their other problems, the fights, he'd thought for sure parenthood would save them, would save her. Quite the opposite had happened. It had been the final, wretched straw. She couldn't stay. She couldn't do it anymore. She couldn't pretend. Freedom was all she longed for, away from England, her father and the expectations that had been foisted on her from a young age. Away from all of them. Away.

"Surely you're interested in Ashley. That kiss is awfully convincing."

How did Joanna talk him into these circles? "She's very pretty. I won't deny that. But she's wrong for me, just like Elle was, and I can't make the same mistake twice. I need solid. Reliable. Sensible. Ashley is none of those things."

"Please promise me you will never, ever set up a profile on an online dating site saying you're looking for a solid, reliable woman. You'll end up with an incredibly loyal lumberjack." She took the seat next to his, reaching over and touching his arm with the tips of her fingers. "Marcus. I want you to be happy. God knows you deserve it. Please just ask Ashley out to dinner. Thank her for the nice thing she did for our business. It's not a big deal."

Everything in Joanna's voice said how much she pitied him, and he hated that. Part of him wanted to ask Ashley out, try again, at least apologize for last night. The rest of him was certain he didn't have time to spend on a date with a woman he'd never end up with. And that was assuming a lot. Ashley had every right to want his head on a platter. "She'll probably say no."

"You won't know until you ask."

His mind flew back to last night—the look on Ashley's face when he'd left her alone in her apartment. "No, I'm certain the answer will be no."

Eight

Ashley stepped off the elevator and came to a stop. Normally she'd head straight for her apartment on the right-hand side of the vestibule. Marcus's door was directly opposite. The two were separated by a thirty-foot expanse of the finest marble floor, a fussy old chandelier and a sea of differing opinions.

I promised Grace. If she was going to ask him to dinner, she should probably do it in person. Calling or texting from across the hall seemed juvenile. She was a grown woman, for God's sake. A grown woman did what she needed to do, no regrets, no second thoughts about rejection. Still, she was drawn to the idea of going home. It would take a lot to prop up her busted confidence after last night.

She inched closer to his door, casually leaning in,

craning her neck to see if she could hear what might be going on in there. It was dead quiet, of course. Marcus loved his calm and quiet. She raised her hand to knock but stopped herself. It was after seven. Maybe this was a bad time. Maybe it was Lila's bedtime. Or her bath time. Or story time. Not that Ashley would know anything about Lila or her routine—Marcus had kept the most precious thing in his life, the reason he couldn't or wouldn't take Ashley seriously, as far away from her as possible.

Ashley did an abrupt about-face. Her purse went flying, as did her metal travel coffee mug, which clattered and clanged across the marble floor. She shushed the damn thing as it noisily collided with the wall. She scrambled to collect her things, then rushed to her door. She was shoving her key into the lock when she heard Marcus's door behind her.

"Ashley?" he asked.

She froze. Her shoulders rose to her ears. Why did that have to be his effect on her? Why did his voice make her behave like a smitten idiot?

"I heard a noise."

"Marcus. Funny running into you." She turned, and his presence hit her like a tidal wave. She was still so hurt from last night, and seeing him felt as though she'd scraped a fresh wound. The problem was that her inclination was to fold herself into those arms of his, not run away and hide, even when he'd had the gall to suggest last night that feelings like that for him were foolish.

"Is it? Funny, I mean? We do live across the hall from each other."

She shook her head, trying to wrench her thoughts away from the kissing variety. How she wanted to kiss him again. Just one more time. Just so she knew it hadn't really been that amazing. It was her womanly due diligence. One ordinary kiss and she'd know it was okay to walk away from Marcus Chambers. "It's been a long day, Marcus."

He shoved his hands into his pants pockets. With his shirtsleeves rolled up to his elbows, the move only served to torment her with his muscled forearms. "Oh. Sure. I'm sorry. I wasn't sure I extended a proper thank-you for last night. That's all." He closed his eyes for an instant. Was it actually painful for him to grant her a single gracious thought?

Thank me for what? The party? Or the part where you told me how wrong we are for each other, only after we got naked together? She nearly clamped her hand over her own mouth to keep the words from coming out. Regardless of how she felt about last night, trying to dish it back to him would only make things worse. She'd have to ask him to dinner some other time. A decade of waiting seemed about right. It simply hurt too much right now. "You're welcome."

He pursed his lips and nodded. "Okay, then. Good night."

"Night." *Bastard.* She rushed to her door and collapsed against it when she was inside. A strong smell of varnish hit her nose, but apartment renovations were the last thing on her mind. She never should've invited Marcus to the premiere. Things weren't merely strained between them now. They were stupid.

She padded back to her bedroom, which felt like returning to the scene of the crime. If things hadn't been in such disarray in the living room, she would've slept on the sofa last night just so she wouldn't have to smell Marcus on the pillows. She kicked off her heels, rubbing her tired feet and ankles, then slipped out of her skirt and blouse and dressed in yoga pants and a tank top. Finally. A tiny measure of comfort.

Her stomach growled. No big surprise considering she'd scarfed a protein bar at two that afternoon and eaten nothing else. She'd had a ridiculously busy day, just like she did every day. She longed to slam on the brakes, just for a few days, but there was no stopping the *Manhattan Matchmaker* train. Not now. Not when the network was seriously considering *First Date in Flight*, a crazy idea Ashley had for a show where couples would have their first date on a cross-country flight. Not when she had a massive online dating site asking her to do commercials for them. She had to strike while the iron was hot. Her kind of good fortune was never long-lived, and she wasn't about to let her family down, ever. Nor was she about to let down Grace, which meant she still had to find a way to get Marcus to dinner.

She ate cold leftover lo mein straight from the carton. The kitchen was progressing nicely with gorgeous white custom cabinets and a gray quartz countertop. The white glass tile backsplash was installed, but there was still wiring hanging out of the outlet junction boxes. For today at least, her apartment was moving forward. No complaints from Marcus. Tiny victories. She'd have to take them.

She tossed the takeout container into the trash, grabbed a bottle of water from the fridge and retreated to her bedroom. Climbing into bed, she made a point of putting the television remote out of reach. According to the clock on the cable box, it was only two minutes until the start of her premiere.

That left her with a book that wasn't holding much interest and her phone. Should she call Marcus and get it over with? Text him? The thing was, she didn't really mind asking the question. It was the dialogue that would surely follow. She could hear it now. *I told you last night that it's a horrible idea.*

Her phone lit up with a text from Marcus. She nearly went into cardiac arrest. Are you awake?

She frowned at her phone. What in the world could he want?

It's 8. I don't go to bed this early.

Can we talk?

Again she had nothing in the way of pleasant facial expressions for her phone. If he was about to hurt her, again, she was done. Absolutely done.

About?

An invitation.

An invitation to what? Step into a boxing ring? Less than twenty-four hours ago, he'd used her pride as a punching bag.

Well? he added.

Yes. Just call. Her phone rang a few seconds later. "Hey," she said, with a voice so sultry and warm she wanted to slap herself. She was just making things worse.

"I know you must be getting ready to watch your show. I won't keep you long."

"I believe the more pressing question is, are you going to watch my show?"

"I don't watch television at night."

"Ah. Likely story." She shifted in bed. "And no, I'm not watching my show. I never watch it. I can't stand to see myself. And my voice. Ugh. I don't like that, either."

"Why don't you like your own voice? I like mine."

"Well, of course you do. That's hardly fair. Pitting a Southern accent and a British accent against each other isn't fair at all. I'll never win."

She heard strains of the *Manhattan Matchmaker* theme song through the phone line. The vision of Marcus watching her show materialized before her.

"You're watching my show. I can hear it." She'd never been in his apartment, so she had to make up that part. Was he sitting in the living room, maybe watching with the ultimate fans in his household, the nanny and housekeeper? Or had everyone gone home for the day? Was he doing what she was doing, curled up in bed, dressed in pajamas? Boxer shorts?

"I've got it on right now. I can see why you don't like your voice."

She sat up in bed and did the unthinkable—she grabbed the remote and turned on the TV. "What's that supposed to mean?" She cringed a bit every time she had to watch herself on screen. She couldn't fathom what it would be like to be a film actress, to have to watch herself on the giant screen.

"It's not so much your actual voice. I like your real voice. It's the one on TV that doesn't sound quite right. It doesn't sound real."

She smirked and sank farther into the pillows. His voice was a definite weakness of hers. She'd better not tell him how much she'd be willing to give up if he asked her in the right tone. "Well, the whole thing isn't really real. The matchmaker part of it is real, and the couples are real, but the rest of it is just a show. That's not even my real office." She pointed at the screen as if he were in the room.

"It's not?"

"Nope. It's a real therapist's office, but not mine. Mine has horrible light, and it's too small to get all of the camera equipment in there."

"Interesting. Although I'm not surprised. These shows all seem to be so contrived. I guess that's why I haven't watched your show more than in passing. My nanny and housekeeper have it on all the time, though."

She didn't really care to continue on this path, the one where Marcus went on about the ways in which he thought her show was idiotic. "What do you want, Marcus?"

"Oh. Right. I called you."

"You did," Ashley answered.

Just come out with it, he thought. Either she was going to say no and he'd have to tell his dad and Joanna to move on to greener pastures, or she'd say yes and he'd spend an entire evening ignoring his attraction to Ashley for the sake of pleasing his dad. He cleared his throat. "I want to thank you for taking me to the party. It gave us an incredible boost in business, and it couldn't have come at a better time."

"So my silly show actually helped you?"

He fought the grumble that wanted to leave his throat. "Look, I'm sorry if it seems like I don't take what you do seriously. Clearly a lot of people do, and I'm thankful for that."

"Careful, Marcus. You almost didn't insult me right there."

He deserved that. He deserved whatever she cared to dish up to him.

"And remind me someday to show you how seriously I take my job."

He watched as her show returned from a commercial, a long shot of her walking down a crowded sidewalk, eventually arriving at what he now knew wasn't really her office. The TV version of her was nice to look at but had nothing on the real Ashley. Just across the hall, all alone. Actually, thinking about the layout of the two apartments, he was fairly certain their bedrooms butted up against each other. *Like I need more torment.* He fought the urge to ask what she was wearing, although he wanted to settle on the fabricated image of her in an oversize T-shirt and sweatpants. That made it easier to have this conversation, but his idiotic mind kept picturing her in a tiny tank top and yoga pants. "I'm sorry, Ashley. How many times do I have to say it?"

"I don't know. I sorta like the ring of it. I'll tell you when to stop."

He deserved that, too. "I'm sorry, okay?"

"Okay."

Just ask her. "I was calling to do more than apologize. I wanted to see if you'd like to see what sort of mileage we can get out of being seen together one more time."

"Really?" Her voice was oddly hopeful.

"Yes. Why did you say it like that?"

She blew out a breath. "Because the network wants us to be seen together again. I was supposed to ask you the same thing, but I was dreading it."

"Is that why you were lingering in the hall earlier tonight?"

"Maybe…"

He had to smile at her precocious nature, and the fact that he wasn't completely stuck with a losing hand. Ashley was in the same predicament. "So I take it that's a yes?"

"I think we should go to dinner, yes. But I'm going to ask you questions at the restaurant, and you have to promise me you'll answer them."

"In the course of normal conversation, I hope."

"I'm not making any promises. All I'm saying is that if you and I go out to eat, I want to be able to talk. For real. About stuff. I think you owe me that much after last night."

Stuff. Once again, he deserved that. They'd be out in public. He could likely handle whatever she had to launch at him. Then he could appease his family and set Chambers Gin on a highly successful track. All he had to do was share a meal with a woman he couldn't keep his hands off, while counting on their natural dynamic to remind him that they were not a good match. "I will accept the grand inquisition. Eight o'clock tomorrow night?"

"Fine. Are you going to arrange a car or shall I?"

"I'll drive."

"You'll what? You have a car? In the city?"

"You heard me, Ashley. I'll drive."

Nine

"You're insane. You know that, right?" If Ashley had known she wouldn't get car sick, she would've closed her eyes. Marcus was treating the streets of Manhattan like his own personal racetrack. "I don't think I know anyone who has a car in the city. If they do, they use it for getting out of town, not going to dinner."

He made another dangerous maneuver with the car, cutting off a city bus. She was scared out of her wits and more than a little turned on.

"Ah, but I'm not insane. One could argue that it's insane to get into a car and let a stranger drive you all over the city. At least I'm in control."

She shook her head. "Most people at least drive a car in the city that can stand some abuse. I don't know what kind of car this is, but it seems like one

ding in the bumper and you'll end up with a huge re-
pair bill." Her fingers caressed the leather upholstery.
Whatever he was driving, it was fast and expensive.

He caressed the steering wheel, reminding her just
how much she liked his hands. "It's an Aston Martin, and believe me, she can take all kinds of abuse."

Photographers were waiting for them when he
pulled up in front of the restaurant. Grace had done
her job letting everyone know that Ashley and Marcus
would be making their second appearance. The valet
opened her door, and Marcus climbed out of the car.

"Take very good care of her." Marcus smoothly
slid a bill into the valet's hand.

"Give us a kiss," one of the photographers shouted.

"Yeah. We need a kiss," a second added.

The others followed suit, asking for the thing that
had thrust Marcus and Ashley's fake coupling into
the public consciousness.

Marcus glanced over at her, unfairly dashing in a
black suit even when he was giving her his most per-
plexed look. He took her hand. Was he going to go
for it? She might have to slap him. Or kiss him back.
She remained undecided.

"It's your call," he said.

Her call. She was too torn between what everyone else wanted *from her* and what she wanted *for
herself*—the chance to show Marcus that she might
not be the perfect woman, but she wasn't the wrong
one, either.

Unfortunately, her body knew precisely how this
should play out. Her cheeks flushed with warmth at

the persistent, almost embarrassing urging from the photographers, from Marcus's penetrating gaze as he towered over her. The photographers wanted the kiss. Her mouth sure wanted the kiss. It even looked like Marcus wanted it, too.

She had to test him. She had to know what he was thinking. "I think we should do whatever you feel like doing."

"Perhaps we should wait." He leaned closer and whispered in her ear, "We can't give them everything at once, right?"

The unusually warm night air brushed across her bare shoulders. Marcus's question made her even hotter, even when he'd just disappointed her greatly. "Right. Keep them waiting."

Inside the restaurant, it felt as if all eyes were on them as they checked in with the hostess. Ashley should have been used to this by now, but it still made her uncomfortable, even after three years of it. She reminded herself that tonight was to make Grace and the network happy, although that wasn't much comfort. The last time she'd tried to please them, she'd done incredibly well, all while setting her own heart on a course for destruction.

They were guided to their table, dead center in the restaurant. *Great. Dining in a fishbowl.* "Do you have a corner booth available?" Ashley asked the hostess.

"Something more romantic. Of course." The hostess turned and led them to a much quieter, more intimate spot.

Ashley's heart sank as she slid into the small

candlelit booth. She consulted her menu while she berated herself. How could she be so stupid? Marcus was probably thinking that she was clinging to romantic notions, which was the last thing she wanted. "What looks good for dinner?" she asked, making small talk since she hadn't mustered the courage to ask him the questions she'd threatened to ask.

He closed his menu. "The steak." He smiled half-heartedly.

The waiter came by and offered a respite by taking their orders for dinner and drinks. Unfortunately, he didn't stay long.

"Look, Ashley, I'm sorry about the other night." Marcus adjusted his flatware on the table, avoiding eye contact. "Things went too far. That's all I can say. I think it's better that I yanked us back from the precipice before it got to be too much."

"Always the gentleman." Why did his logic so often end with a case of horrible frustration? Why did it actually have to hurt?

"It's the only way to be with a woman."

Be with a woman. Ashley's entire being bristled with curiosity over Marcus's love life, the sorts of women he'd been with, especially his ex-wife. "Since you made it clear that we're wrong for each other, I want to know what you look for in a woman. I think you owe me that much after the other night."

He nodded solemnly, taking a deep breath, seeming stuck in his thoughts. "It's not the same now as it was when I was younger. Lila changed all of that. I need a woman who wants to be both wife and mother."

"That's it? Nothing else matters?"

"Of course other things matter, but it's not that easy to quantify it. I only know that I want at least that much. It hasn't been easy. It's a delicate balance to let someone into your life only once you're certain that it's a good idea."

"But you let me into your life. Was that a good idea?"

He took a long sip of his drink, eying her with an intensity that set her on edge. "You pushed your way into my life. There was no letting you anywhere."

Her stomach knotted. Why did he see her as the veritable bull in a china shop? It made her feel like such a clod.

Out of the corner of her eye, Ashley saw a woman approaching the table. She had a piece of paper and a pen in hand.

"I think someone's coming over for my auto-graph," she whispered to Marcus.

"Really?" He glanced back over his shoulder. "Oh. So I see."

"Ashley, I'm your biggest fan," the woman said, trembling as she inched closer to the table.

Marcus's expression said that he was truly embar-rassed. This made Ashley want to invite the woman to join them.

Ashley scooted over on the banquette seat and pat-ted the cushion. "What's your name?"

"Michelle. Can I have your autograph?"

Ashley took the piece of paper and scrawled her signature, personalizing it and adding a bit about hoping she had a life full of true love. "I hope you enjoy this. It was very nice to meet you, Michelle."

Tears began to stream down the woman's cheeks as she looked at what Ashley had written. "My boyfriend broke up with me. I don't know why. I thought he was the one, but I guess he wasn't because he left."

Marcus noticeably bristled, and Ashley shot him a look. This poor woman was hurting so badly that Ashley could feel the pain square in the middle of her chest. Breakups were always the worst kind of heartache, the kind that felt permanent, a life sentence, like it would never go away.

Ashley rummaged through her purse for a tissue and handed it to Michelle. "Sometimes we have to be with the wrong ones just to help us learn what we want out of a partner."

Michelle nodded, wiping the tears from her cheek. "It just feels so hopeless right now. I feel so hopeless. I don't even know what to do. I walk around this city all day long like a zombie and I have to just smile and go to work and pretend I'm not feeling any of it. I hate it."

Marcus stood. "You ladies will have to excuse me." He stalked away. Everything in his body language said that he was annoyed. Ashley wasn't sure where he was going, and she wasn't entirely sure that she cared.

Ashley thought back to the months after the breakup with James. He had made her feel so important at first, as if she truly belonged in this unfamiliar world of money, stature and fame. He'd propped her up and helped her see her own worth. Just as easily, he'd torn her down, claiming that she'd led him on since she wasn't ready for marriage. She wasn't ready for children. He didn't care that she felt so overwhelmed by her life that the idea of marriage and children just made her stressed out. And for that, she'd been turned into a zombie, just like Michelle, forced to smile and do her job while her heart crumbled into tiny pieces.

She had to help this woman. Without hesitation, she pulled a business card out of her purse and handed it over. She wouldn't normally give her contact information to a fan, but this was important. "Tell you what. I want you to go on the show's website and fill out the dating profile and an application to be on *Manhattan Matchmaker*."

Michelle's tears made a swift reappearance. "Really? I've heard it's practically impossible to get on the show."

Ashley smiled wide. These were the moments she lived for, when she had a real chance to help someone. "And that's where my card comes in. Send me an email when you've done it and I'll have the producers move up your application."

"Really?"

"No promises, but we'll give you the best chance possible. If there's a match for you in our database, I'll find him."

"You're being so nice to me. I don't even know what to say."

"You know what, Michelle? I'm helping you because I know exactly how you feel. Exactly."

Marcus waited for the water in the sink to heat up, glaring at his reflection in the men's room mirror. Why was he so annoyed? Why did the interruption of the woman bother him so much? Was it because it was outside normal, polite behavior? Or was it because this was a powerful reminder of what Ashley's life was like and what she was comfortable with—the unexpected, the out of control?

Thankfully, the woman was gone by the time Marcus arrived back at the table. Their entrées had arrived, as well. He shook out his napkin and took his seat.

"Well, that was interesting." He wanted to let it go, but he couldn't.

"What was?" Ashley twirled pasta on to her fork and popped it into her mouth. A tiny bit of noodle poked out from between her lips, and she sucked it in. Her lips—why did they have to speak to him like that? Even when he was angry with her, she could do these sexy things that stopped him dead in his tracks.

"The interruption of our meal."

"It was just for a few minutes, Marcus. It's really not a big deal."

"I don't understand how you stand it."

"She was crying. What was I supposed to do?" She

leaned forward and whispered, "Tell her to shove off because I was on a date with my fake boyfriend?"

A sputter left his throat. "Don't call me that."

"Oh, I'm sorry. My disgruntled neighbor."

His brain said that he was her embattled neighbor. As she gathered her hair in her hands and twisted it to the side, draping it over her shoulder, his body said he was her horribly frustrated neighbor. "And I wasn't asking you to get rid of her, but you also didn't have to listen to her entire life story. That seemed excessive."

"She needed someone to listen to her, she sought me out and I wasn't about to turn her away. This is what I do, Marcus. I counsel people. I help them find love. I help them understand the things that are keeping them from love."

He certainly felt put in his place. "You actually take this seriously when the cameras aren't on?"

Her eyes grew impossibly large. "You do realize I'm actually qualified to do this, right? I Googled you and you couldn't be bothered to do the same? After all this time?"

"I'm not nosy. And it's none of my business."

She shook her head and returned to her pasta. "I'm a licensed professional counselor, Marcus. I was a clinical counselor for years before the matchmaking show came about. I've clocked a lot of hours listening to people tell me how unhappy they are, especially with their love lives."

"How in the world did you get a television show out of that? You must have really pulled some strings."

Her shoulders dropped with exasperation. "The

show was an accident. I had two clients who I was sure were perfect for each other. So I arranged for them to meet by accident in my waiting room."

"That hardly seems ethical."

"It probably isn't, but you know what? They're married with two kids and incredibly happy, so I don't regret it for a second. My female client figured out what I'd done, and she was immensely thankful and grateful. We had a talk about matchmaking, and I told her that I'd been doing it since I was a kid."

His vision narrowed. "You what?"

"My first match was in fifth grade. My best friend, Elizabeth, and a boy named Sam. They just seemed like they belonged together, but they hated each other. I was signed up to help the teacher after school on the same day as Sam, but I pretended to be sick and got Elizabeth to do it instead. They were boyfriend and girlfriend the next day."

"Don't tell me they're married with two kids."

"No, they're not. But they were each other's first kiss. And they actually ended up friends, so I didn't do too badly the first time around. That was the start of it, and once I realized I was good at it, I just kept doing it."

"And that's how your face ended up on the side of half of the buses in Manhattan?"

"I knew my client had a production company specializing in reality TV, but I never dreamed she'd ask me to do a pilot for a show. That was not my aim."

"Your aim was to help your clients fall in love?"

"Yes. It physically pained me to think about how

perfect they were for each other, knowing they might not ever meet. It wasn't right."

Marcus swallowed. He'd read Ashley wrong on this point. She really did take this seriously. And her goals were noble. There was no question about that. "Sometimes people might seem like they're perfect for each other, and it can be quite the opposite in reality."

"Let me guess. Your ex-wife."

He should have seen that coming.

"Remember, I did my due diligence on you, even if you didn't do it on me." She set her fork down on the table and took a sip of her wine. "So tell me. What happened?"

He looked around the restaurant, although for what he wasn't sure. Now he almost wished one of her rabid fans would turn up and interrupt them. "It's a long story. You don't want to hear it. Trust me."

"I told you I was going to ask questions tonight. That's my first question."

"Let's just say that we thought we were perfect for each other, but we weren't."

"And? What else? That's not a long story. That's not even a short story."

He could only imagine what it must be like to have Ashley as a therapist. She did seem as though she'd be good at dragging things out of people. "Elle and I met the summer after I graduated from university. One of the things that drew me to her was that she seemed to need me. I'd never really experienced that before and it felt good. She was eager to get married and she latched on to me tightly. It wasn't until we got married that I realized she'd really just hoped to get away from her family, especially her father."

"Was there some sort of abuse going on?"

Marcus shook his head. "No, but her parents were very controlling. I never got to know them well because she always kept her distance. Honestly, they were never anything but polite to me, so I didn't really have a way of knowing. As soon as she was out of their house, being with me was no better, apparently. I realized very quickly that everything made her feel tied down. Every social obligation, everything she was expected to do. It really weighed on her."

"And she took it out on you."

For a moment, everything in the restaurant seemed to come to a standstill. Visions of Elle flashed in his mind—the two of them up all night fighting until she would eventually leave. That was always her inclination—to leave. "Yes."

"When people break free from one thing, they often just find something else they want to break free from. It becomes a pattern, and a strong one. It can be difficult to break because they don't know how to function any other way."

He already felt choked up at what came next—the most painful part, the thing that told him the marriage had to come to an end. "I thought a baby would help. I really wanted to start a family, and I figured that love is what makes people want to stay where they are. If she didn't love me, surely she would love the baby."

"And it made it worse."

"It did." He finished off his drink, hoping to numb the pain. "She hated motherhood. I think she loves Lila on a basic level, I truly do, but she just wasn't cut out to be a mom. I'm sort of amazed that she was ever able to admit that. She didn't sugarcoat it when she left. She simply didn't want to be with either me or Lila."

Ashley nodded, intently focused on him. She reached her hand across the table. "Marcus, I am so sorry. Truly. That must have been so hard." Her fingers looked tiny wrapped around his hand. Her thumb rode across the ridge of his knuckles, bringing up his bounty of conflicted feelings. Attraction warred with sensibility. Something even more primal than that battled his need to remain on an even keel. This was more than he'd bargained on, but then again, everything with Ashley was far more than he expected. "You know, we can't always predict how things will go. It's so obvious to me that this was a very painful chapter in your life, but at least she brought you Lila."

Marcus narrowed his stare. "And she completely ruined my life. She brought all kinds of embarrassment on my family and left Lila without a mother."

"And she broke your heart."

"That's the one concession I won't make. I won't give her the satisfaction." The reality was that Elle had done more than break his heart. She'd stolen his faith in love. He'd thought love could save him, could save *them*, but it wasn't the unwavering, all-powerful force people deemed it to be. Love changed. Love faded away.

Ashley held up her finger. "You know, I think you're stoic and stern because you're hurt. Everything that your wife did to you, I'm not sure you've dealt with. You're holding on to so much hurt. I can see it in your eyes. You have to learn to let it go or it will eat you alive. I might even suggest you see a therapist. Finally start talking about your feelings."

He pressed his lips together, stifling any verbal response. Between Ashley and Joanna, he was getting pushed from all sides—*deal with your feelings, find the right woman.* Why did life have to be so complicated?

"I don't want to diminish what you've been through, but Lila was meant to be your little girl and she had to get on the planet somehow. Don't discount the good parts in that."

He took in a deep breath, staring into what was left of his gin and tonic, swirling the ice in the glass. Indeed, Lila had to get on the planet somehow. As much as Elle had taken from him, she'd given him Lila, his entire reason for living. Ashley did have a point. Even so, he didn't care to go on about it forever. "We should go. The nanny is watching her this evening, and I did promise I'd be home by eleven."

Marcus held the door for Ashley as they left the restaurant. The photographers were waiting for them.

"How about it, you two? Can we get that kiss now? We've been out here for hours."

Marcus was still in a haze over the things Ashley had said to him about Elle, about his marriage. Part of him thought she might be right. Part of him had a strong distaste for the ways she summed up what she presumed were his feelings. It wasn't as simple as she'd made it sound.

Ashley took his hand. "They're waiting," she muttered, nodding in the direction of the photographers. "We should probably just get this over with."

"Hey," one of the photographers barked. "I'm from *Celebrity Chitchat*. Maryann Powell thinks you two are a fake."

Before he had a chance to pop off at the photographer, Ashley's hands were on Marcus's neck, she was up on her toes and her lips were on his. Ambushed with a kiss, something in him snapped. He wrapped one arm around her waist and cupped the side of her face with his other hand, tilting her head back and pulling her against him until her feet left the ground. He kissed her back with no mercy, attempting to rival her impetuousness, match her reckless nature. He was too wound up now. Too frustrated by everything in his world that demanded a fight.

He set her back on the ground when he'd made his point. Ashley was breathless. Her chest heaved. "So much for fake."

Indeed, the photographers were all grinning and stowing their cameras. The valet zipped Marcus's Aston Martin up to the curb. He walked in the direction of his car, unsure he had the strength to make it back to their building. So much for fake, indeed. *I have got to stop kissing this woman.*

Ten

Wednesday nights always meant a family dinner with Joanna, at Marcus's apartment. Lila loved her aunt Joanna, and Marcus enjoyed the time with his sister away from the business of Chambers Gin. Sales had boomed exponentially after his second public appearance with Ashley mere days ago, when he'd taken out his frustration on her very kissable lips. Marcus wasn't sure which he was more stressed about—sorting his feelings for Ashley or preparing for media night at the distillery.

"This is the last work thing I'll bring up tonight, but we really need to go over the final details for media night on Saturday. It's days away." Marcus was excited by the prospect, especially since they'd had even more media outlets ask for an invitation after the two tabloid appearances with Ashley.

"You worry about your interview with Oscar Pruitt," Joanna replied. "I'll worry about everything else."

"Dad has been waiting on a Chambers Gin feature in *International Spirits* for years. I don't think I could worry any more than I already am." *If I don't dazzle Oscar Pruitt, we're sunk.*

"Please. Marcus. Let's save work for tomorrow." Joanna held Lila's hands and helped her motor across the kitchen floor. "I can't believe how big my niece is getting."

His little girl wasn't far from being a walker. Before long, she'd be toddling all over the apartment, climbing furniture, saying far more than "hi" and "Da." Things were going so fast—too fast. He had to get serious about dating, about finding a mother for Lila. He just needed a bit of time to get past Ashley mentally.

Marcus pulled a shepherd's pie from the oven that Martha, his housekeeper, had prepared according to their mother's exacting directions.

"Do I smell something burning?" Joanna's voice squeaked.

"You do realize that jokes about my cooking aren't going to work, right? I didn't make this."

She scooped Lila up into her arms. "No. I'm serious. I smell smoke."

Marcus set down the oven mitts and stepped away from the stove. That was when the smell hit him, too.

Panic quickly followed. "Is it coming from the hall?" He rushed to the door and placed his hand against it. Still cool to the touch, and no signs of smoke coming out from under it. And yet the smell was there. "Get Lila's diaper bag. And your purse," he barked.

He opened the door slowly. The vestibule was clear, but the smoke smell was stronger. One glance at Ashley's apartment door and he whipped around to where Joanna was standing. "Get Lila out of here now. Take the stairs. It's safer." It was warm enough outside that they wouldn't need coats. He patted his pockets. No cell phone. It was in his room. "Call the fire department on your way down. Now go." He kissed Lila on the cheek, hoping like hell this wouldn't be the last time he'd ever see her or his sister. "Everything's going to be okay, darling. Go with Auntie Jo."

Joanna's eyes were wide with panic. "Marcus, you're coming with me."

"Go. Now. I mean it. I have to make sure Ashley isn't home."

Joanna disappeared into the stairwell with Lila.

He bounded over and began pounding on Ashley's door. "Please don't be home," he muttered to himself. "Please don't be home." Was she in there? He didn't have a phone. And why wasn't the fire alarm going off? He'd have to do it himself. He lunged for the red box and pulled the bar. Without a second wasted, he grabbed the fire extinguisher across from the elevator and returned to Ashley's door. No answer as he pounded the hell out of it.

The cycling squeal of the alarm was deafening, but he knew it would be a good half hour before the fire department could arrive. He'd read horror stories of Manhattan fires out of control. He and Ashley lived on the top floor, which would likely keep the fire contained, but the nagging question of whether Ashley was inside her apartment wouldn't leave him. He couldn't go. Not until he knew for certain she wasn't home.

He touched the doorknob with the tips of his fingers. It wasn't hot. Ideally the fire wouldn't be too bad. He stood back and kicked the door with every ounce of adrenaline he could. The force of the kick rippled up through his heel and into his leg. It hurt like hell. Still, the door refused to give. He kicked again. And again. And again. Finally it flew open. Smoke was everywhere inside Ashley's apartment, but it wasn't so heavy that he couldn't see. He took a handkerchief from his pocket and placed it over his mouth, then crouched down and went inside.

"Ashley!" he yelled from behind the cover over his mouth. Smoke billowed out of the kitchen. He stepped closer and saw the flames. He took aim with the fire extinguisher hose, surprised by the force with which the chemicals came. He sprayed back and forth across the base of the fire. Luckily it only took a moment before it was out. It had been contained to the kitchen, but it wouldn't have been long before it would've engulfed the rest of the apartment. What would have happened if Joanna hadn't smelled the smoke? He didn't even want to think about it. After a quick look in the other rooms, he ran into his apartment, grabbed his cell phone and headed downstairs.

He placed a call to Joanna while he raced down the eleven flights. "Are you and Lila out?"

"Yes. We're in a cab right now. What's happening?"

"The fire's out. It was a few minutes from being really, really bad."

"Oh my God, Marcus. Get out of there. Get in a cab and stay with me for the night."

"No. You keep Lila. It will make me feel a lot better if she's safe with you until the fire department can check out the building. I have to call Ashley and tell her what happened." He could only imagine how devastated she'd be. "Do you need anything?"

"I have plenty of supplies from the last time Lila stayed with me. Her diaper bag has a change of clothes. We'll be fine."

Joanna bid her goodbyes as Marcus filed out of the lobby with many of the other residents, who were all wondering what happened. Marcus found Mrs. White and filled her in.

"Good Lord, Mr. Chambers. Ashley will be so upset. It's a good thing she can just move into your apartment now that you two are an item."

He painted a smile on his face. "I have to call her right now. Can you speak to the fire department if they arrive while I'm on the phone? Excuse me." He separated himself from the crowd of people outside the building, placing the call to Ashley, jamming his finger in his ear. "Please answer, please answer..." he muttered as the phone rang.

"I hope you aren't calling to complain about my contractor. I've had the worst day."

Her voice sent a surprising wave of relief coursing through him. She was okay. The fire was out. Lila and Joanna were safe. "I'm so sorry to tell you this, Ashley, but there's been a fire."

A fire. No. No. No.

Ashley had never so frantically hailed a cab in all her life. She yanked a twenty-dollar bill from her wallet and flattened it against the Plexiglas between her and the taxi driver. "This is your tip if you get me home, now."

"Yes, ma'am." The driver looked over his shoulder, punched the accelerator, dodged another taxi and ran a red light.

She eased back in her seat and wrapped her arms around her waist, rocking back and forth. Deep breaths seemed impossible. Every drag she took of oxygen only teased her lungs before being quickly expelled. "It's going to be okay. It's going to be okay."

She stared out the cab window, but she didn't see the city. Instead, visions of the fire that took her family home when she was ten years old overtook her mind. She couldn't push them out no matter how hard she tried. She saw it all, she *felt* it all—standing in the ditch next to Rural Route 4, the dusty road that ran past her family's farm. Faded, splintered clapboards that her great-grandfather had hammered into place by hand went up like scrap wood in a bonfire. Licks of fire swallowed the living room curtains her mother had sewn from bedsheets. It was as if they'd been nothing, made of tissue. Every last one of their belongings—furniture, their clothes, her most treasured books, the diary she'd been keeping for only a few weeks, the teddy bear she'd had since she was a baby—all of it had been taken that night. For good.

The loss had been enormous and in many ways, her family hadn't truly begun to heal from it until Ashley landed the matchmaker show and started making real money. Then she'd been able to lift her family out of debt, buy her parents a house, give her brothers a little something extra. The fire had led to more than a decade of struggle that the entire family was ill-prepared for, especially Ashley. She'd had to grow up overnight. The thing was—before the fire, she hadn't given much thought to being poor.

The farm had been such a happy place—thriving crops in the fields, a garden chock-full of yellow wax beans and tomatoes, chickens chattering in the yard next to the henhouse, barn cats sleeping in the sun on the front porch. The house was paid for. Her great-grandfather had built it himself. Before the fire, it had always felt as though they had plenty, or at least enough. After the fire, the henhouse was the only thing left standing, and there was no insurance, no money for a motel. They'd depended on the kindness of neighbors to help them through it.

And once again, things were tumbling down. By the time Ashley got up to her apartment, the scene was strange—both quiet and busy. Three or four fire-fighters milled in and out of the door. The heavy smell of smoke became stronger with her every step forward, until it began to sting her nose and stopped her dead in her tracks. If she stayed out here in the hall, it didn't have to be real. She didn't have to face what was waiting for her on the other side of her door.

Marcus came out of his apartment. "You're here." His voice was serious, sounding as if it was any other day.

Ashley shook her head, turning and looking up into the complexity of his eyes. "So you smelled smoke? That's how you found it?" With every passing word, her voice grew weaker.

Marcus pulled her into a hug, and she had to work to keep from collapsing in his arms. He made her feel protected, and it was so tempting to give into that, to take it willingly. How had he ended up as her support system? How had this man who could be so insufferable ended up being her saving grace? Even when he'd tried everything he could to push her away.

She didn't have a single safety net in her life. She spent her days walking a tightrope, trying to keep everything going, trying to keep everyone else secure. It was nice to know that someone, somewhere, could make her feel that way. She'd never expected it would be Marcus, nor did she have any idea how he felt about the role.

It wasn't that she couldn't see a way out of this. She'd get back on schedule with her apartment somehow. It would be everything she'd hoped for. But she'd have to retrace parts of her gut-wrenching past to get through it. No wonder she felt as if someone was turning a knife in her stomach.

"Joanna smelled the smoke. She was over for dinner. I had her take Lila. Obviously I wanted her out of harm's way."

Tears stung Ashley's eyes. *Harm's way.* Her apartment was the source of that harm. "You could've been hurt. Little Lila could've been hurt. Marcus, I'm so sorry. Thank God you were here and acted so quickly. Thank you for doing what you did. I'm never going to be able to thank you."

He patted her back and pulled her in for another hug, reminding her she was safe. "The fire marshal should be out any moment now. I don't think you're allowed inside yet. They've cut the electricity, anyway. They seem certain the fire was electrical."

A man wearing a firefighter's uniform adorned with a very important-looking patch came through her apartment door. "I'd know you anywhere, Ms. George. I'm Lieutenant Williams. Very nice to meet you. My wife is a huge fan."

"Oh, that's nice." It wasn't exactly what she'd imagined she would first say to this man. She had dozens of questions, but she couldn't bring herself to ask even one. She stood as still as a statue, bracing for whatever came next.

"I'll have to get an autograph from you at some point, but in the meantime, let's talk about your fire."

Or not. We could not talk about it and just pretend it didn't happen.

"The point of origin was one of the kitchen outlets. My guess is faulty wiring." Lieutenant Williams stepped closer and showed her a photo on his phone. Marcus stood behind her, looking over her shoulder, appraising things with his watchful eye.

One glimpse of the scene and she clamped her eyes shut—her gourmet retreat with the eight-burner stove and custom cabinets now resembled the remnants of a campfire. The gorgeous glass backsplash was marked with a gaping black hole. "The electrician was just working on the kitchen the other day," she mumbled, her stomach sinking.

"Yes, well, we're going to need to speak to your contractor about that. That's why we cut the electricity to the apartment. We don't want to risk another fire. I'll be back in the morning to begin the inspection of your unit. Shouldn't take more than a few days. Then you can get a team in here to clean up. In the meantime, I can't allow you to occupy the space. You can gather some of your items as long as a fire department member is here. Do you have a friend you can stay with?"

Grace was her closest friend, but she lived with her sister and a handful of cats in a tiny apartment. It would never work. They'd all be on top of each other. "I'll find a hotel room."

Marcus cleared his throat but didn't say anything. She wasn't shocked he hadn't offered, but she wished he had. At least it would've made it easier to deal with the fire department. Maybe it was for the best that they stay away from each other. She didn't need more confused feelings heaped on top of the ones she had right now.

"Also, Ms. George," Lieutenant Williams said, "you should know that your sprinkler system failed, and we suspect it was compromised. If your contractor's workers bypassed the system, I have no choice but to file a report with the city. There will be an investigation. They could lose their license. It's a very serious safety violation."

"I don't understand, though. They had a waiting list. Their other work is beautiful."

Lieutenant Williams shrugged. "We see this every now and then, even with some of the best contractors. One worker takes a few shortcuts and everyone suffers."

"There's nobody else who could've done it. They're the only people who have been working in my apartment." Marcus had been right all along. However "in-demand" her contractor had been, she'd ended up with a team of idiots working on her project. She'd given in to tunnel vision, just moving forward with the renovations because all she wanted was her apartment to be done. She'd wanted that one thing for herself, at any cost. "I guess I need to start looking for a new contractor." She disbelieved the words as they left her mouth. She'd been so sure Marcus would be the reason her renovations came grinding to a halt. In the end, it was because the company she'd hired—and defended all along—had done a terrible job.

He nodded. "You should be able to return in a week or so. We won't hold your apartment hostage forever. You're very lucky that Mr. Chambers acted so quickly. It could've been far worse for your apartment and for the entire building. I'd say that all things considered, this is a good thing. You would've been living with a ticking time bomb. That bad electrical could've short-circuited at any time—while you were asleep, while your neighbors were asleep."

The weight of everything threatened to knock Ashley to the ground. *It could've been far worse.* She knew worse. She'd lived worse. She was so relieved that no one had been hurt, but her guilt over the possibility was crushing. She took in a deep breath as tears bloomed at the corners of her eyes. She had to stay strong…at least until she could collapse in a heap on a hotel bed.

Ashley and Marcus stepped away. "It's okay," she said. "You can tell me now that I messed up. I know I did." She waited for the lecture or at least that smug look on his face, the one that would say without words that he was, once again, right. And she had been wrong. Tragically wrong.

"I don't have to say it. It's all quite clear."

She waited for the part about how it was okay that she'd made a mistake, but he didn't say it. And she couldn't blame him. He and his family had been put at risk.

"I'm sorry, Marcus. I don't know what else to say."

"You can say that you'll stay with me," he said. "If you'd like to."

Her eyes narrowed. "Really?"

"Yes. You can stay with me. You can be nearby

while they do the inspection, you can be on hand if your contractor shows up, and all of your things are here. It's the only sensible thing to do."

Because you'd invite me to stay only if it was sensible. "I thought you didn't like to have women around Lila."

"Lila's perfectly safe at my sister's. She can stay there for a few days. I wouldn't dare bring her back into the building until the inspection is complete, anyway. I can visit her before or after work. She'll be safe from all of this."

He nodded in the direction of her apartment, but the invisible line between Marcus and her door went right through her. Her choices had created the danger. They'd prompted Marcus's need to keep the most precious thing in his life far away from her.

"So? Are you accepting my invitation? I'm too tired to persuade you, so you'll have to make the call."

Could she do this? Retreat to the home of the man she'd cursed on a regular basis just a few weeks ago? *Should* she do this? Would they just end up arguing over breakfast? Or would she spend the night staring at the ceiling, wondering what he'd worn to bed that night? "Yes. Thank you. I appreciate it." She turned back to her apartment door. "I really don't think I want to go in there." Her voice was shaky again. She dreaded the thought of seeing the damage firsthand.

"Why don't you get settled in my guest room? I'm sure I can find something for you to sleep in."

"Old potato sack lying around somewhere?"

"Something like that."

They made their way to his apartment. This was the first time Marcus had allowed her to step over his threshold, and she didn't take the invitation lightly. He'd been clear—women who weren't the nanny or housekeeper didn't come over. Of course, Lila, the person he was protecting, wasn't here to protect. She'd been whisked away to safety.

Marcus's furnishings were trim and masculine—a charcoal-gray sofa, chocolate-brown leather armchairs and a low wood coffee table, set against the backdrop of marine-blue walls with crisp white trim, with vintage black-and-white framed photographs and old maps as art. A massive basket in the corner overflowed with colorful toys, a happy oasis in an otherwise sophisticated and serious room. She followed him down the hall, where he flipped on the light in his extra bedroom. "I trust this will work."

This room was serene refinement in soft white and shades of cream, camel and café au lait. "It's perfect. Thank you." She took in a deep breath. There was so much to do—deal with insurance and the fire department, get everything cleaned. And then there was her contractor. Clearly the crew had to be fired tomorrow. As to whom she'd hire to finish things up, it was back to the drawing board. She had another year of celebrity under her belt since she'd last contacted her first-choice builders. Perhaps they could be persuaded to move her up in the queue.

"I need to find you something to sleep in," he said, sounding a bit uncomfortable with the task he'd given himself. "I'll be right back."

"That would be great." Ashley sat on the edge of the bed, exhausted and struggling to get a handle on her feelings. The fire was a living nightmare, but it had landed her in Marcus's inner sanctum, a place she'd been fairly sure he'd keep her out of forever. It was hard not to be fascinated by this glimpse into his life, to see a glimmer of hope. She and Marcus Chambers might have horrible odds romantically, but there was still something about him that left her wanting more.

He reappeared in her doorway, presenting her with a pair of pale blue, perfectly pressed men's pajamas. "I, uh, I don't know what you normally wear to bed, but I hope this will do."

She had to smile at his sewn-up approach, knowing that when the lights were turned down and clothes were coming off, he was uninhibited and commanding. Regret over their almost-night together still ate at her. If only they'd actually made love, if only she'd been able to witness the moment when he unraveled, she would have had another piece of the sexy, complicated puzzle standing before her. "Is this what you normally sleep in?" she asked, raising an eyebrow at the pajamas.

"Just the pants. I can't stand to wear a shirt to bed."

A flood of heat and frustration threatened to consume her. He'd just plopped a sequence of half-dressed images in her head that would be hard to shake, especially knowing it was all going to play out in the next room in a few minutes. All night long.

"You wouldn't want to smother yourself with pajamas."

He knocked a knuckle against the door frame. "I'll leave you to it. I'm sure you want to phone your family."

Her family. Good God, she hadn't dared to entertain the notion. It would crush her mother. Her dad might not handle it much better, and he needed to avoid stress at all costs. Why did reality have to encroach on her daydreamy thoughts of Marcus and his chest? "I'll call them tomorrow."

"Are you sure? I don't know what I would've done without my family after Elle left. They got me through everything. I really think you'll feel better if you talk to them now."

And there it was—another piece of the puzzle, willingly given. He wasn't afraid to admit that he'd needed help and support during his divorce. So he *was* human after all. "Yes. You're right. I promise to call them first thing in the morning. I'll let them get their rest tonight."

Eleven

Marcus might have wished Ashley a good night's rest, but he'd had nothing of the sort. If he was torn over how he felt about her before, he was even more conflicted now. The adrenaline rush of the fire, coupled with missing Lila, all while perseverating on the image of Ashley in his pajamas, had left him restless all night.

Yes, Ashley had created the situation that put Lila, his sister and the entire building in danger last night. He'd told her dozens of times that her contractor was reckless and irresponsible and she'd refused to listen. But then again…he couldn't fathom her leaving them on the project if she'd had any idea what would happen.

He'd seen it the night they went out to dinner. She

wasn't self-centered, nor was she dumb. Carefree and audacious? Yes. Brazenly negligent? No. Did that leave her as the victim? Probably. Which was precisely why he couldn't let her go to a hotel last night, even when it meant subjecting himself to the physically arduous proximity of being around a woman he knew he was falling in love with, even when he'd sworn he wouldn't.

Realizing he'd claimed as much rest as he could possibly get, he climbed out of bed and took a shower. Getting into the office early was the best way to deal with the way she made him feel. When he'd given her his pajamas last night, he'd been fighting every urge imaginable—to take her in his arms, kiss her, admit to panicking the night of the premiere and ask for a second chance. To make love to her, if only to be able to stop the talking, the endless back and forth, and physically express how he felt. He might not be able to put his feelings into words or coherent thought, but he was fairly certain he could put them into action.

Last night, she was stuck in this unthinkable situation and had been so vulnerable, but still remained strong. How she'd kept from truly breaking down was beyond him. There had been shaky moments, there had been tears, but that was it. Had she been putting on a good face for him? Or had he actually managed to comfort her?

The rattle of dishes and closing of cabinet doors came from the kitchen. Better to get used to running into his new roommate now, rather than avoiding the situation. He sauntered down the hall but wasn't ready for the vision that greeted him—Ashley on her tip-toes in nothing more than the shirt from his pajamas, searching through the kitchen cabinets.

He coughed, partly to get her attention, partly to keep himself from walking up behind her and snaking his arms around her waist. He *did* have a good ninety minutes until his sister expected him in the office. They could accomplish a lot in that much time. "Good morning."

She dropped back down to bare feet and turned. Her hair was a sexy mess. She didn't have on a lick of makeup—still beautiful, but in an entirely different way than he was used to. "You're up. Is there coffee?"

"Sorry. Just tea."

She frowned, making her chin wrinkly, which was surprisingly cute. "You have got to be kidding me. How am I supposed to function?"

Reaching past her, he opened the cabinet where he kept the tea bags. He set one of the boxes on the counter then filled the kettle with water. "There's plenty of caffeine in English breakfast tea."

"Wait a minute." She pointed at him, shaking her finger while he turned on the stove burner. "I know you drink coffee. I've seen you come up to the apartment with a to-go cup."

"I do drink it, but I don't make it. Never learned how." He got out a mug for her as she leaned against the kitchen counter, resting one of her bare feet on top of the other. Her legs were almost more tempting now than they'd been the night of the premiere.

He knew everything her legs led to. "So, what's on the schedule today?" he asked, consulting his watch, distracting himself.

She folded her arms across her chest, causing the nightshirt to hitch up and the side vent to split open, revealing an edge of some sort of pale purple temptation. "I have a million things to do. I already talked to the insurance company. They're sending an adjuster over this afternoon. I heard from the fire marshal, and he already has one of his men working over there. I can fetch my stuff anytime I want. Suffice it to say, I won't be going into the office today. Which is fine. I need a break."

"Do you want me to go with you across the hall to get a few of your things? I know you weren't up to it last night, but you can't live in my pajamas all day long." *If you did, I might be forced to take the day off, too.*

"No. It's fine. Lieutenant Williams is going to be here in an hour. I'll wait and go in with him."

Great. I'll leave her with a handsome, strapping fireman. "Ah, well, then. I guess I'll just get off to the office. Martha, the housekeeper, will be by later this morning to clean and prepare dinner."

Dread nagged Ashley as she looked at her phone. She didn't like the idea of burdening her mother with anything, especially bad news. In fact, she took it as her personal charge to bring only good news. *They renewed my show for another season. I'm sending more money.* She hadn't even shared the news about James dumping her until she'd flown home for Thanksgiving last year, and cracked the instant she saw her mom. Considering the fact that a story about Ashley's fire was in the newspaper and making the rounds online that morning, she didn't have a choice. It was time to be the bearer of bad tidings.

Her mom answered on the third ring. "Hey, baby girl."

"Hi, Mama."

"It's nearly nine thirty. It's not like you to call me from work."

Ashley's eyes drifted shut. Her mother's warm, syrupy drawl brought her to tears, but she had to choke them back. She had to be strong, just like she'd been with Marcus last night. She wasn't about to burden her mom unnecessarily. "I'm not at work. I'm taking the day off."

"What happened? You never miss work."

And to think she'd worried that crying would rat her out. Her mother knew something was amiss just because her workaholic daughter wasn't in the office. "Something happened with my apartment, but I really, really don't want you to worry." She couldn't bring herself to say the word. She couldn't force herself to say *fire.*

"Not something with that neighbor of yours, is it? I thought you two were dating."

Crap. She hadn't bargained on her mom knowing about that. "Did you see that in the papers?"

"One of your brothers emailed me a link. I figured

you'd call me and tell me what was going on when you were ready for me to know."

"We aren't really dating. It's complicated." *Beyond complicated.* "We were in a position to help each other's businesses. And we're trying to be friends, but we argue a fair amount. He doesn't like my contractor. I don't really know what's going on between us, to be honest."

"You're rambling, darling. And you still haven't told me what happened with your apartment."

Ashley took in a deep breath. "There was a fire."

"Oh no." There was such finality to her mother's words. "Are you okay? You weren't hurt, were you?"

"I'm fine. Really. Actually, my neighbor Marcus was the one who discovered the fire. He put it out and everything. Before the fire department arrived."

"Please tell me you weren't home."

"I wasn't. I was at work."

Her mother exhaled deeply. "I have never been so thankful for that crazy job of yours. Are you going to be okay? Do you need to come home for a few days? Let me feed you and you can sleep in and we'll have our girl time."

Ashley smiled. Just a few minutes of talking to her mom had lowered her stress level dramatically. "I would love to do that, but I have to stay and deal with the fire marshal and the insurance company and find a new contractor."

"Okay, honey. I know you're busy. I just want you to know that we're here for you. Always. I'm sure that the fire was a scary thing, considering everything that happened when you were a girl, but you need to recognize that good things come out of bad, too."

"What good came out of that fire? It was all bad."

"Actually, a lot of good things happened. It made your father quit smoking. Another decade or two of that and we probably would have lost him to a stroke long before now. Plus, your dad and I weren't doing that well at the time. Running the farm was hard, and it was driving a wedge between us."

"It was?" Ashley sat back against the headboard. "You never told me that."

"You were ten years old. And that was between your father and me. Some things have to stay between a husband and a wife. Nobody else needs to know. Regardless, the fire brought us closer. We realized how much we needed each other. It made the financial problems that came after it much easier to handle."

"I think of that time as being so hard."

"It was incredibly hard. But your father got me through it. That's what love does, darling. It makes all of the bad tolerable. You should know that better than anyone. You go to work and find a lot of people true love."

"Not that I'm actually able to find it for myself. That would make too much sense, wouldn't it? For the woman who searches for love all day to actually find it for herself?"

"So tell me what the situation is with you and Marcus."

If only her mother knew what a long conversation this could end up being. "There is no situation.

I mean, I liked him a lot at first, but then I thought he didn't like me."

"And now?"

"Now, I don't really know what to think. He has a very complicated life. I'm just not sure I'm up for that. He's had a hard time, went through a really painful divorce and is trying to raise his daughter on his own. I'm starting to see why he can come across as a jerk. He closes himself off to everything."

"Just like you do."

For a moment, Ashley wasn't sure of what she'd heard her mother say. "What? I don't do that at all. You know me. I'll talk about anything."

"Maybe when it comes to other people. You close doors when you don't like what you see. You've done that since you were a little girl. If something bad happened, you just learned to ignore it. You were always better at helping other people than helping yourself."

Ashley's mind flew back to the palm reading in the limo. She didn't really believe in that stuff, but Marcus had said virtually the same thing of her. *Oh my God. She's right. He's right.* She'd closed the door on the bad behavior of her contractor. She'd closed the door on the fire, trying to put on a brave face for Marcus so he wouldn't see her fall apart. She'd closed the door on the reasons James had left. Why wasn't she ready for a real commitment? For children?

"Mama, can I ask you a question?"

"Of course."

"Do you think I'm too scattered to be a good mom or wife?"

Her mother laughed quietly. "Didn't I just get done saying that you're better at helping others than helping yourself? That's pretty much the first requirement of being a wife and a mom. Being scattered has nothing to do with it. And you're not scattered. You're full of life. You aren't afraid to take on new things, even if it stretches you a little bit."

"I'm not afraid to take on new things if I think I'm going to be good at them."

"Or if it helps you help someone else."

She hadn't thought about it that way, but that wasn't far off base. She'd taken on the matchmaker show not completely certain she'd do well at it, only knowing that she had to take the chance so she could help her family.

"So, Ashley Anne, do you like him?"

"Who? Marcus?"

"The man in the moon. Of course I mean Marcus."

Ashley instructed her clients not to think when she asked them questions like this. It was a time for the heart to take the lead. "I do. He can be a big mystery, but I feel like I find out something new every time we spend time together. I just keep going back, even when things aren't going well, because I'm dying to know more. I guess you could say he has me hooked."

"And does he like you?"

"I'm not sure, to be honest. I mean, he invited me to stay at his apartment, so I'm pretty sure he doesn't hate me."

"Sounds to me like you need to find a way to his heart. And you know what that means."

Ashley smiled wide. "You think so?"

"Absolutely. You need to cook for the man. That's the surest way to figure out how he feels."

Twelve

Mama had given her marching orders—cook for the man. A homemade, South Carolina low country, George family dinner. Shrimp and grits—the kind of dinner her mother would have made when there was money for groceries. For dessert, a coconut layer cake, six layers, the way her grandmother had made it. Ashley knew every step by heart.

But first, clothes. The black pencil skirt she'd worn to work yesterday was fine, but the smell of smoke had permeated her silk blouse just from twenty minutes out in the hall. She hoped Marcus would feel okay if she borrowed one of his dress shirts for a little while. She'd take it to the cleaners when she was done with it. Plus she wanted to see his bedroom.

When she rounded the corner into his room, she

was greeted with masculine splendor, much like the rest of the house. A tufted brown leather headboard crowned the head of his bed. A white duvet and pillows topped it with a gray wool blanket cast aside. The bed was still unmade, a rumple of sheets. Of course—the housekeeper would be by soon.

Ashley couldn't help it—she crept over to the side of the bed and turned, perching precariously on the edge of the mattress. Her hand smoothed over the silky sheets. Damn him. He *would* have to buy bedding with a high thread count. Probably the finest Egyptian cotton. She knew she shouldn't have been doing it, but there was something so comforting and cozy about sitting where he'd been sleeping mere hours ago. More than comforting—it was a bit titillating. His naked chest and back had touched these sheets. The morning after he'd rejected her, she'd forced herself to wash the memory of him from the bedding.

Atop a gorgeous wood chest next to the bed sat a white-shaded reading lamp, an alarm clock and a silver-framed photograph of him and Lila. She was probably only a few months old in the picture, the two of them nose to nose, her tiny, dimpled hands touching his face, the two of them grinning. Their mutual adoration was so evident it made Ashley's heart ache. They'd been through so much. Together. There had to be days when Marcus felt as though it was just he and Lila against the world. After these many months, would he even be able to make room for a woman in their lives? Would he trust another woman with not only his heart but also the heart of his sweet little girl? Marcus's protective tactics made one thing clear—he'd risk his own heart far before he'd risk Lila's.

She ventured into his closet, a shrine to meticulous organization. The man would probably pass out if he ever saw the condition of her closet, bursting at the seams with dresses and shoes—good God, the shoes. She thumbed through his shirts, admiring a few, finding a French-blue one that didn't look like it was too horribly expensive. Except that it was probably incredibly expensive. She slipped into it, buttoned it and rolled up the sleeves. With some creative tucking to make it look less like she was swimming in a shirt, she headed back down the hall.

Noises came from the kitchen—the housekeeper.

Ashley marched over and held out her hand. "Hi there. I'm Ashley. You must be Martha."

The woman's bright blue eyes were wide with surprise. "You're the matchmaker. I watch your show all the time." She dropped the towel she was using to wipe the counters, her hand flying to her face. "You had a fire. I saw the firemen in the hall just now. I'm so sorry."

Ashley nodded. "Yes. Thank goodness it wasn't a total loss. I'm headed over there right now. I need to get a few of my things and try to see about getting everything fixed up."

"You aren't going to have the same builder come back, are you? They were horrible."

Ashley sighed. Why had she been so stupid? "I

know that now. I'm so sorry if they were an inconvenience for you."

Martha picked up her towel and ran some water in the sink. "I just don't like to see Mr. Chambers get so upset. He works very hard and he's a great boss. He gave me two weeks off with full pay when my husband had back surgery. He even had meals sent to our apartment."

Now that she knew Marcus, she shouldn't have been even the slightest bit surprised that he would do something like that. "That was very generous of him."

"He's a good man. A very good man. And his daughter is an angel. Of course, he protects her like he's a bear, but that's what a father does. Especially when she doesn't have a mother."

Ashley wasn't sure whether she should feel better that Martha's information confirmed that her feelings for Marcus were warranted, or if she should feel like she might never match up to his epic goodness. He clearly had a generous heart. He just hid it from a lot of people.

"Well, you don't need to worry about preparing dinner for tonight," Ashley said. "I'm taking care of that. I want to thank Marcus for all he has done for me."

Martha's face lit up. "How nice. I'm sure he'll love it."

Ashley retrieved clothes, toiletries and several pairs of shoes from her apartment, rushing through the whole thing as quickly as possible. She had to escape the smoke smell—it was everywhere. She didn't even go into the kitchen. The pictures had been enough. She had her talks with Lieutenant Williams and the insurance adjuster out in the hall, then returned to Marcus's apartment and threw everything in the wash. She left a message for the new contractor she hoped she'd be able to hire this time around, then embarked on her shopping trip, managing to remain under the radar for most of it, having to stop only once to take a quick photo and give an autograph.

When she returned to Marcus's apartment, she changed into jeans and a tank top, getting right to work by first putting the cake layers in the oven. Memories hit her the minute the sweet fragrance of that golden sponge cake began to fill the kitchen. Every breath took her closer to home…the sticky South Carolina summer, magnolias and honeysuckle, and crisp air in the fall. It seemed so far off. Too far off. Part of her longed to be back there, to be plain old Ashley George, no cameras or billboards or publicity photos. It was nice no longer to struggle the way she had back at home, but those struggles had been replaced by new ones, the most profound of which was the nagging sense that she had money and a beautiful, charred apartment, but her life had become empty. She had no one to share this life she had built. And she had to wonder if she was sabotaging herself by still holding on to romantic thoughts of Marcus when so much pointed to the idea that they didn't quite fit together—different personalities, divergent situations. If she were giving herself love advice, if she'd been the woman crying in a restaurant about a broken heart, she'd say that it might be the smart thing to move on. The problem was, she'd tried, and the only thing she'd learned in the process was that she had no talent for giving up on Marcus.

After carefully slicing the cake layers, she assembled the cake and gave it the finishing touches, pressing coconut to fluffy white cream cheese frosting—her mother's twist on her grandmother's traditional seven-minute icing. She stood back and admired her handiwork. The grits were cooking away on the stove, the shrimp and other ingredients prepped and waiting for Marcus to arrive home so she could throw it all together at the last minute.

He walked through the door and for a moment, she felt as self-conscious as could be. Was he going to think all of this was silly? Unnecessary? And why did he have to look so incredible after being at work all day? She usually looked as if she'd been run over by a train.

"What's all this?" he asked, surveying the kitchen and loosening his tie.

She gave the grits a stir and turned back to him. "I gave Martha the night off. I'm making you dinner."

"And there's cake?" He swiped icing from the base of the plate.

"Hey. That's for later."

He flashed his green eyes at her. Every time he did that she suffered a bout of amnesia. It was impossible to remember a single bad thing that had ever happened between them. "Do I have a minute to change clothes?" He pointed at her. "From the look of things,

I'd say I'm overdressed. Plus, I can't wait to get out of this suit."

Out of this suit. That mental image was going to stick with her for a while. "Of course."

She's making me dinner. And how lovely the sight of her in his kitchen was after a hectic day at the office. He knew better than to think that this would be a normal occurrence if he and Ashley were a couple. She'd be busy with work. He'd be similarly occupied. But it was a nice fantasy.

He quickly changed into jeans and a Cambridge Rowing Club T-shirt. *Much better.* Wearing a suit to the office was one of the worst parts of his day. "It really smells incredible." He approached Ashley from behind as she worked at the cooktop.

"Almost ready to eat. I just need to finish up the shrimp."

"Is it okay if I open a bottle of wine? I trust a white will work with the meal?"

She nodded, wiping her forehead with the back of her hand. "Yes. Perfect."

He fetched the wine and two glasses, filling them just as she was spooning the meal into shallow bowls.

"Ready?" he asked, nodding toward the dining area.

"I'll meet you in there."

The table was set perfectly with placemats and linen napkins, and she'd thankfully had the sense to put them at one end, next to each other. She'd even dimmed the chandelier overhead. He couldn't escape the romance of it. Was she being kind? Or did she see the opportunity he was so eager to take? He really wanted the chance to redeem himself, or at least to know for certain whether they had any business being together.

"No candles?" he asked.

"Considering what happened yesterday, I thought it best we avoid fire." She set down his plate before him and took the seat next to his.

"Smart." He laughed quietly, holding up his wine glass. "A toast to everyone being safe and sound."

She gently clinked her glass against his. "Thank goodness."

He took a bite of the meal she'd prepared—succulent sautéed shrimp with bacon and scallions atop a cheesy, creamy substance that closely resembled porridge. "This is delicious. What is this mixture at the bottom of the dish?"

"They're grits. I'm guessing you've never had them."

He shook his head "Not once. They're good."

"It's dried, ground corn. Put in enough butter and cheese and you'll think you died and went to heaven. I practically grew up on them. They are, as my mother would say, dirt cheap."

He studied her, considering what she'd said. "Is she a real bargain shopper?"

"She is, but it was a necessity, too. We never had much money and things got a bit dire after we had a fire."

Now he was even more confounded. "No. A fire?"

She nodded and looked at him with an expression

much like the one he'd seen her wear last night—
vulnerable, but strong-willed. "Yes. We lost our house
to one when I was ten."

His heart seized up in his chest as she told him
the story. Her family lost everything. It led to years
of struggle. He couldn't fathom that particular loss.
She'd had such a potent reminder of it last night.
Reaching across the table, he grasped her hand. The
gesture was forward and intimate, but it was his only
inclination. "I'm so sorry, Ash. I can only imagine
what was going through your mind last night."

"Last night is still a blur, but yes, it brought back
a lot of bad memories. I don't like to think about it
too much or it'll just make me sad. Nobody wants a
sad houseguest."

"You can be sad if you want to. You should allow
yourself to process it."

"I'll process it a lot better once I meet with my
new contractor on Monday."

"Ready to jump back in already?"

"I have to move forward." She shrugged. "I called
the builder that I couldn't get the first time around.
Turns out their new office manager is a fan of the
show. They've made room for me in their schedule.
I made a bank transfer of ten grand for the deposit
this afternoon. I guess that much is good."

"If they treat you well and do a good job, then
yes." It hit him then—the reason she'd been so stub-
born about her renovation. "No wonder you're so at-
tached to your apartment. You lost your home when
you were a girl."

She pushed the food around on her plate with her fork. "That's a big part of it. When you grow up with nothing, especially not growing up in one place, you attach a lot of meaning to the idea of home." She stopped speaking, seeming deep in reflection, then looked at him. "The apartment also means a lot because it's the only tangible part of my success. Everything else about what I do is like air. It's not like what you do. You make gin. You can hold on to a bottle of gin. Most of the time what I do doesn't even seem real to me."

That's what she'd been doing all that time he was waging war against her. She hadn't been wrapped up in material goods. She'd been defending her big-city, eleventh-floor homestead because it was the only thing she had. "I had no idea. You really should have said something. I knew you were from South Carolina, but the way you carry yourself, I had visions of money and a grand Southern home."

A quiet snicker left her lips. "You watch too many movies. Scarlett O'Hara is a fictional character. And besides, she lived in Georgia."

"What about your parents now? Has life gotten any better?"

"It has. With my job, I can finally help them financially. My dad had a stroke about five years ago, and my mother takes care of him full-time, so they need it."

"No siblings to help?"

"I have two older brothers, and they help when they can, but they both work construction and have families. I just happened to be lucky enough to get a job that pays me more money than is probably reasonable."

He was glad he wasn't keeping track of the many ways in which he'd misjudged Ashley. He'd be losing, big time. "You're an industry, Ashley George. I've witnessed it. Don't diminish the appeal of you." All he could think about was how great her appeal was to him. He wanted to kiss her so badly it was as if the devil was on his shoulder berating him to just do it.

Warmth colored her cheeks in a breathtaking rush of peach. "It's very sweet of you to say that. I don't understand the idea of me as an industry or appealing, but I'll take it."

"The thing that amazes me is how you manage to do everything you do. How do you fit it all into one day? You spend an awful lot of time taking care of everyone else." A lump caught in his throat, one he found hard to get past. "I have to wonder who takes care of you."

"I could ask you the very same thing."

"I suppose you could."

She took another sip of wine. "Now that I told you my whole life story, I feel like you have to tell me a little more about yours. Let me guess. You grew up in a castle."

He laughed quietly. "Talk about watching too many movies. It was more of a Victorian townhouse in London. But it was a comfortable upbringing. I can't think of a major trial in my life until, well, you know. Lila's mother leaving us." To his surprise, uttering the words didn't bring the normal stabbing sensation in his chest. It was liberating to say it out loud and not feel crippled by it.

"No wonder it hit you so hard. The first time you encounter a big trauma in your life and it ends up being a doozy."

He couldn't help but notice how healing it felt to talk to Ashley, to have someone who knew his sad story *really* listen to him. She didn't have an agenda outside trying to understand him better. "Indeed it did."

She gathered her napkin in her hand and placed it next to her plate. "I should probably get to the dishes or it'll be an hour until we can have cake."

He got up from the table and took her dish. "I'll help. We do not want to delay the arrival of cake."

Ashley began collecting pots and pans while he loaded plates and cutlery into the dishwasher. He hadn't done dishes in quite a long time, but he would've dug a ditch if it meant the chance to watch Ashley bend over and put a pot back into the cabinet. Eventually he ended up with his hands in hot, soapy water, scrubbing the cooking vessel for the grits while Ashley ran to the bathroom. He couldn't stop thinking about the moment when he'd taken her hand at the table and she hadn't flinched at all. He couldn't stop thinking about the ways in which he'd read her wrong. He definitely couldn't stop thinking about the urge to kiss her.

"Almost done?" Ashley asked, returning to the kitchen.

He pulled the drain plug from the sink and rinsed that final pot, leaving it to air-dry. "Last one. And it's a good thing. I was beginning to prune."

"Let me see," she said with a comedic air of concern. She took his hand and turned it over in hers. "Oh, you don't look too bad to me. I think you'll live." She peered down at his hand, not letting go. She dragged her finger along the head line. "Is this the heart line?

He smiled, especially when she stepped closer and he could inhale that beguiling summer rain scent of hers. "That's actually the head line. Mine says that I'm a quick thinker. It also means I draw conclusions quickly. It's not a good thing."

"Hmm. I think I'm familiar with that aspect of your personality." She inched her finger across his palm. "What about this one?"

"Life. Mine says that I need to learn to relax."

"Either you're making it up, or this is ridiculously accurate." She moved her finger to the final line to be read.

"That one's the heart line." He leaned back against the kitchen counter, not about to relinquish his hand, unsubtly pulling her closer. Her touch was driving him crazy in the best possible way, bringing every inch of him alive.

"And what does your heart line say?" she asked.

He didn't want to tell her the truth about his heart line. It said he'd experienced a deep, personal betrayal. It wasn't that he was over it—he didn't want to dwell on it with Ashley anymore. They both had their scars. "Why don't you tell me what you think it says?"

She looked up at him and bit her lower lip, leaving his poor heart to jackhammer in his chest. Her impossibly warm and welcoming eyes scanned his face, back and forth, taking in everything. "I'd guess that it says you have a big heart. A generous one."

He placed his other hand on her waist, tugging her closer, stepping to the edge of a precipice he'd visited many times. He couldn't walk away from her if he started something. It wouldn't just hurt her. It would mark him for life. "It actually says that I'm a bloody idiot if I don't kiss the incredible woman standing in my kitchen."

She smiled and rolled her eyes. "That's the oldest trick in the book, Chambers."

He threaded his hand into her hair, anticipating the kiss he was about to plant on her sweet, pink lips. "It's not a bad one, either."

Thirteen

Marcus's kiss was an arrow straight to the heart. Dinner was apparently the best idea ever, judging by the way he was kissing her. She tilted her head to the opposite side, taking another approach. She pressed into him so hard, his head thunked against the upper kitchen cabinet.

"Oh my God, Marcus. Are you okay?"

His eyelids were heavy and sexy as if he'd just woken up. He whipped her around, pushing her butt up against the kitchen island. "Yes. I'm sure I had that coming at some point in our friendship." His lips were on hers again, his tongue toying with hers while one hand went up the back of her top, unhooking her bra. His other hand was flattened against her back, pressing her into him, erasing any space between them.

She was exploring the landscape of his back beneath his impossibly soft and worn T-shirt. Every muscle was so defined, so articulated, just begging to be read by her fingers. She couldn't wait to do the same to the front of him.

She leaned back and tugged his T-shirt up and away. "You're so damn sexy in a pair of jeans. I'm struggling to comprehend it."

"Remind me to wear them more often."

She unhooked his button, needing him out of these clothes. Part of her was so eager finally to have him. The rest of her was just hoping to hell that he wasn't going to make her stop. There'd be no coming back from that. She lowered his zipper.

"Or not," he said, swallowing hard. "I don't have to wear the jeans if you don't want me to."

He pulled off her top, adding it to the pile of clothes on the kitchen floor. Next went her bra. "Please tell me you have a condom readily available this time," she said.

"Or what?"

"Or I might have to withhold cake. And I'm definitely withholding sex."

He took her hand and pulled her down the hall. "Good thing I have a whole box. I'm hoping I get to have both cake and sex."

She giggled as they walked into his bedroom. It was so different this time, knowing she was an invited guest—she wasn't sneaking around. He wanted her there. He wanted her, period. She could see it in his eyes.

He gripped her rib cage, caressing the undersides of her breasts with his thumbs, all while practically peering into her soul, peeling away every layer she covered herself in. Making her naked, making her his. He took off her jeans, wiggled her panties past her hips, looking at her. Connecting with his eyes. Making it clear just how serious he was. For once, she was glad he was being serious. Really serious.

He threw back the covers and pulled her down onto the bed, but she had one more bit of business before they could go any further.

Kneeling between his legs, she shimmied his boxers down his hips. He was so ready and magnificent, it was hard to comprehend. Did the man have any shortcomings? She looked at him again. Definitely not. "I haven't touched you yet, Marcus."

"I'm aware of that."

"I didn't have the chance that night."

"I don't want to think about it. It's too painful."

She drew a finger up the center of his thigh, from his knee to the deep contour along his hip, causing him to buck off the bed. "Do you want me to touch you now?"

He propped himself up on his elbows. "Yes. Please."

She lowered her head, huffing warm air against his length. "What about now?"

"You're torturing me, Ash. Please just do it. I'm begging you."

She didn't want to make him beg at all. That wasn't her aim. She just wanted it to be incredible, and she knew it would be so much better if he felt like he'd had to wait for it. The anticipation would make the reward that much sweeter. She gently reached out, taking him in hand and wrapping her fingers around him.

He growled like a bear—a big, happy bear. "That's it."

She caressed his length, up, rolling her palm over the tip, down to the base, tightening her grip as she went. She observed every reaction, making note of the things that made him want to watch, the things that made him close his eyes and roll his head to the side, the things that made his lips part in ecstasy. She loved having this small measure of control over him, pleasing him, knowing that at that moment, she could give him everything he wanted.

He sat up and rolled her to her back, resting his full body weight on her, his thigh rubbing between her legs. The pressure was immense. It made her light-headed. "I can't wait any longer. I have to be inside you." He pushed her hair from her face tenderly and kissed her—a soft, wet kiss.

"Make love to me," she replied. Funny how things between them in the bedroom were so effortless. At least this time.

He sat up and opened the drawer of the chest next to his side of the bed, pulling out the foil pouch, ripping it open and putting it on. He crawled over to her as if he was hunting her. The anticipation made her knees knock to the side, opening herself to him. No more hiding. No more barriers.

He came inside, and she waited for the moment when

everything would become blurry and the world would fall away. But being with Marcus was different—no hazy, dreamy state. No—this was strong, pulling her into the moment, demanding her presence.

"Look at me, Ash." He thrust forcefully, deeply, but he was in no rush. Quite the opposite. "Tell me what you need."

She shifted herself a tiny bit, and that left his pelvic bone to rub against her in the perfect spot. She pulled her knees higher, enjoying every sublime inch of him as he rode inside and out. She moaned softly. "That's perfect. Stay right there."

He sank down against her, adding to the pressure, kissing her deeply and passionately. Her hands traveled across his strong back, found his incredible ass, gave him a good grab to let him know he was everything she needed. Each thrust brought her closer to the edge. She felt her insides tightening, coiling, about to spring at any second. Her breaths became short and staccato. Marcus's did, too.

"I'm so close," she said, meeting him with her own force.

"Me, too. You feel amazing, Ash."

She smiled and nestled her face in his neck, closed her eyes, her muscles contracting faster, stronger. He matched her intensity and she clutched his body, grabbing him with everything inside her, calling out. He followed soon after with a gruff rumble from the depths of his throat.

Still inside her, keeping her close, he rolled to his side and took her with him. He kissed her forehead dozens of times. She felt so adored. It wasn't the after-the-fact cuddling she'd expected from Marcus. "That was fabulous," he said. "I'm so sorry I made you wait, but I hope it was worth it."

She sighed, drinking in his smell, his presence. She'd fantasized about this moment with Marcus, but to her great surprise, her own, very active imagination hadn't come close. "It was worth it more than you know."

Ashley woke before Marcus did. He was so gorgeous while he was sleeping, she could have stared at him for hours. But she really needed a glass of water, so she rolled out of bed quietly and crept into the kitchen. Her phone was sitting on the counter and she picked it up out of habit, but as soon as she saw the text from Grace, she really wished she hadn't.

Maryann is out to get you, I swear. Can you get Marcus to go somewhere with you? So we can shut her up? Let me know so I can leak it. I hope you're well. Missed you at work yesterday.

Following the text was a link to Maryann's wretched website. The headline read, Manhattan Matchmaker and Brit Boyfriend a Sham.

Marcus's steps came down the hall, and he approached her from behind at the center island, gripping her shoulders and kissing her neck. "Good morning."

His kiss caused such a pleasant vibration, it almost

made her forget the thing with Maryann. She loved hearing those two particular words delivered with his incredible accent. "Morning, definitely. Good is up for debate, but you kissing my neck makes it a lot better."

He put a kettle of water on the stovetop. "I thought last night was magnificent, but if you want me to try harder, I just need some tea and breakfast. Maybe do some push-ups." He winked and leaned against the kitchen counter.

Who knew he had a goofy side? She never would've seen it if things hadn't happened the way they had. "Our friend Maryann has decided to strike. She wrote a story saying we're fake. She says that you kicking down my door during the fire is proof. If you were my real boyfriend, you would've had a key. Or at least that's what she claims should be obvious to anyone with half a brain."

"That cow." Deep crinkles marked his forehead as he rounded the island. He stood at her side, quickly slipping his warm hand beneath the hem of her tank top.

"Marcus, you can't go around calling people that. It's awful."

"Sorry. It's a Brit thing. It's really not that bad back at home." He scanned the article, shaking his head. "She's trying to steal my heroic thunder. It's not every man who can kick down a door, you know."

"I still can't believe you did that. Remind me on Monday to talk to my contractor about a stronger door."

"Funny. Very, very funny." The kettle whistled, rattling on the gas cooktop. Marcus turned off the heat and filled two mugs, dropping a tea bag into each. "And just because we're a couple doesn't mean we've exchanged keys. It doesn't even mean that we're shagging."

"Nobody's going to believe that. Any woman would have to be crazy not to try to get you into bed."

"Is that so? Are you going to show me how sane you are by seducing me this morning?" he asked, hitting an earth-shatteringly low register with his voice.

"Right after we figure out what to do about this."

"It's very simple. I have the media night at the distillery tonight. Come with me. We already know how to put on a show for the cameras. I'm sure we'll be even more convincing now. We've had practice." His eyebrows bounced, prompting her to laugh.

"It's not a bad idea, but considering recent events, I hadn't exactly planned on going out tonight. I have nothing to wear. My fancy dresses all smell like smoke."

"Nothing a little shopping can't fix." He placed a mug of tea on the counter in front of her. "It'll be great. We'll show everyone just how much of a couple we are."

Ashley didn't like slapping labels on things like relationships, but the question begged to be asked. "Is that how you see us? As a couple?"

His eyes locked on hers, ramping up her nervousness. His hand went to her hair, looping it behind her ear. "Do you subscribe to the idea that things happen for a reason?"

"A little bit, but it's also my job to give fate a nudge. I'd be a hypocrite if I said I believe fate is entirely in control."

"It just seems to me that the fire was exactly what you and I needed."

She thought of everything her mother had said about good coming from bad. If the most recent fire hadn't happened, she'd be across the hall, alone, living in the proverbial ticking time bomb. It was the best possible thing to happen to her, to them. "It gave us a chance to be together."

"Under circumstances that made us both comfortable. If we were to make a go of things, we would need time together. Alone. Like a normal couple. The fire has given us that chance."

Normal couple. Could they be that? He seemed to be hinting at that, but she still suspected Marcus would risk his own heart far before he'd risk Lila's. She couldn't blame him in the least. "I'd like to make a go of things." *Because I'm falling in love with you.* She couldn't bring herself to utter those words, even though they were precisely what sprang to mind. She couldn't say it when things were so new. Not when she was certain he wasn't anywhere close to returning the sentiment. The words tumbled around in her head, her heart beating so oddly she trembled. Perhaps it was because her heart knew exactly how much there was on the line with Marcus. She had, after all, vowed to protect her heart after James, and here she was, so eager to leave her heart without a safety net.

And even if their alone time went well, she still had her biggest obstacle to face. Was she ready to take on motherhood? Could she manage the one part of this that was absolutely nonnegotiable? Could the scattered woman with the insane job and crazy life be what Marcus needed? If she took it on, she couldn't walk away. He'd suffered the pain of that once. She'd have to be one hundred percent sure she was the right woman, and how would she know that unless Marcus let her in completely? Until he let her spend time with Lila?

"Good. I'd like to make a go of things, too." He smiled so wide it made her heart sing. Now was not the moment for dwelling on everything that could go wrong.

"It takes two sides to build a bridge."

He wrapped her up in his arms and planted the softest, steamiest kiss on her. "I hope you don't care if our tea gets cold. I'd like to spend some time working on our bridge before I have to go to work."

Fourteen

The time had come for Ashley to shut Maryann the hell up.

That meant the time had also come for her to get ready to go on her real date with Marcus, to the media night for the new distillery.

They hadn't seen much outside the four walls of his bedroom since he'd come from work Friday night, although they had run out hours ago to buy her a dress. Getting lost in each other was too sublime a temptation to otherwise worry about the outside world or even basic necessities like eating, although Marcus had encouraged the consumption of coconut cake when possible.

Things between them were wonderful and effortless for the moment, albeit very up in the air. Lila would be returning Monday morning, and the plan all along had been for Ashley to move back into her apartment that day. Her new builder would be coming in then to get her project back on track. As for what the future held, Ashley wasn't about to venture a single guess.

Ashley stepped into the shower in Marcus's bathroom.

"Can I watch?" He peeked around the corner while stepping into his suit pants.

"Not if you want to be on time to the biggest night ever for your business." She stuck her head beneath the spray and lathered her hair with shampoo.

"Now who's the grump?"

"I'm just being real with you, Marcus," she called before he disappeared.

She put on her makeup and headed into Marcus's closet. The dress she and Marcus had shopped for that afternoon was hanging there. She unzipped the silver garment bag, removing the black satin gown. She still wasn't sure she had the nerve to wear it. Marcus had come just shy of drooling when she'd stepped out of the fitting room.

"We'll take it," he'd said to the saleswoman while handing over his credit card.

Ashley had called him over with a curl of her finger. "You didn't even ask me if I liked it."

"I love it. And I'm paying."

"I have my own money and plenty of it."

He'd glanced over at the counter where the saleswoman was ringing up the sale. "Too late. She already ran my card."

She'd kissed him then—a slow brush of lips as silky as the dress. She'd slinked back into the dressing room, changed and handed the dress over to be wrapped up. Marcus had won that round. She was fine with that.

And now she was slipping into the dress for the second time. Goose bumps dotted her arms and chest as the silky fabric skimmed over her skin. She caught a glimpse of her reflection in the mirror, and the mere thought of Marcus seeing her made her blush. This dress left little to the imagination, even though it was impeccably tasteful. The bias-cut satin moved with her every curve—her hips, her butt, her breasts. She wasn't sure what she would do if Marcus hugged her while she was wearing this dress. She already felt as if she was naked. His hands on any part of her were absolutely going to send her over the top.

She slipped into a pair of heels and pulled her hair up into a twist. He'd said that he liked it when she'd worn her hair up at the *Manhattan Matchmaker* party. Had he really paid that much attention? Had he really noticed? It felt good to know that he had—even though that night had ended so badly.

She started down the hall quietly, anticipating the moment when they would lay eyes on each other. Marcus was standing in the kitchen, his back to her. His shoulders were the first thing she noticed—so strong and broad and tempting, especially since she'd committed every naked contour beneath that suit to memory. She inched closer, nervous anticipation making her breaths come out erratically.

He turned, and she was no longer nervous about him appraising her. She was too busy drinking in the vision of him—the long lines of that black suit, his strong jaw, those dark and slightly unruly brows of his. He was mesmerizing. If she was really, truly expected to be a gracious and composed guest this evening, she couldn't be counted on for a solid performance. At some point, she'd surely be caught staring and biting her bottom lip.

He unleashed the most clever smile she'd ever seen, as if he was the sly fox and he'd laid eyes on a sweet, fluffy bunny waiting just for him. She'd be his bunny if he wanted her to be. She'd relinquish all control to him, in the bedroom at least. The rest of their dynamic was not up for grabs, but he had to know that by now.

"You are absolutely stunning," he said in his disarming voice.

Ashley dropped her clutch. Lipstick rolled across the floor. She bent over to pick it up, but Marcus reached for it at the same time. Both of them crouching over her purse, their eyes locked. Well, they locked for an instant. Then his eyes very unsubtly dropped to her cleavage and she just let him look, didn't shy away. She was too busy wishing they didn't have to go anywhere tonight. *Look. Look all you want. Then kiss me, dammit. Kiss me and take off my dress and treat it in a way that makes me feel bad that you spent so much money on it.*

She couldn't say the words on her lips—the poor man had work to do. Later.

"Thank you," she whispered. "I have to say that you in that suit isn't really fair. It's like shooting fish in a barrel."

"Well, now I feel like I can conquer the entire world of gin making."

"Good. That's precisely how you should be feeling."

He smirked and straightened, putting an end to their close-to-horizontal meeting of the minds. Ever the gentleman, he held out his hand, helping her back up to standing.

"We should get going. Don't want you to be late." Ashley led the way to his door.

"That dress should probably be illegal," he quipped as he trailed behind her.

She stopped and turned. "Technically, it's yours, Chambers. I'm completely innocent."

"It would be worth every minute in jail."

They took the elevator downstairs to the parking garage and the waiting limo. It was a half-hour ride to get out to the distillery in New Jersey. The time flew, mostly because she was perfectly content to hold hands and just be with him. They went for stretches without talking, the quiet almost comforting to her. Marcus, however, seemed to become more anxious with every passing mile. He tapped his knuckle against the window, staring out as the world whizzed by them.

"Nervous?" she asked.

He nodded. "I am. I'm excited for the company. I just want to make my dad proud. I need to nail the interview. He's waited a lifetime for Chambers Gin to be featured in the magazine. It's a big break. Well, I mean, aside from the *Manhattan Matchmaker* premiere. That was a big break, too."

"No, I get it. The interview is a big deal. You'll do great."

"We'll see. I tend to clam up a bit in these situations. I don't enjoy having to sell myself. I'd prefer the gin do the talking for me."

They pulled up outside the distillery, a large industrial building, not quite the locale for her killer dress. But tonight was about Marcus, which meant making him happy, and apparently the dress did exactly that. They climbed out of the limo and were greeted by a handful of paparazzi. Grace had, once again, done her job—the photographer from Maryann's website was there.

"Hello, everyone," Marcus said, taking Ashley's hand as the photographers snapped away. "Don't stay out here too long. All of the excitement's inside. Feel free to join us for a nip of Chambers No. 9."

He then slipped his arm around her waist and kissed her cheek, his warm lips remaining for a moment and leaving behind a lasting tingle. Part of Ashley's coming tonight was to show up Maryann, but she couldn't escape the feeling that there was more behind that kiss, something that went beyond sex or putting on a show for the cameras. There was something very protective about it, as if he was holding on to her, tightly.

Ashley knew Marcus's sister, Joanna, the second they stepped inside. She had Marcus's presence— tall and ridiculously eye-catching, just a much more feminine version.

"Jo, this is Ashley," Marcus said.

His sister swatted his arm. "Of course it is." She swallowed Ashley up in a hug. "It's so wonderful to meet you. Marcus has told me so much about you." Amusement crossed her face and she glanced at her brother. "You're right. She's even more gorgeous in person."

Ashley didn't know what to say. She merely side-eyed Marcus.

"I'm nothing if not honest," he said.

Joanna took Ashley's hand. "Come on, Ash. I'll take you into the central tasting room so we can mingle with the press. Marcus has Oscar Pruitt waiting for him."

"He's waiting?" Marcus asked, an urgent edge of annoyance in his voice. "Bloody hell, Jo. Why didn't anyone tell me?"

"Don't be such a tosser. You were already on your way when he arrived. I got him settled in the tasting room a few minutes ago. He made it clear he expects a private tour of the facility, just the two of you, but don't worry. I'll keep everyone out until you're done." Joanna patted him on the shoulder.

Marcus blew out a breath through his nose. He squeezed Ashley's hand and pecked her on the forehead, but his stress level was evident. "Enjoy your-self, darling. I'll see you in a bit."

She gripped his arm to stop him before he could walk away. His expression was as worried as could be. "Oscar Pruitt isn't going to know what hit him. You have the best gin in the country, and you know everything there is to know about it. Now go make your dad proud."

He grinned at her, shaking his head in disbelief. "Where exactly did you come from, Ashley George?"

"Across the hall, remember?"

He smirked. "Oh, right."

The central tasting room was buzzing with peo-ple and activity, a dozen or so round, high-topped tables with upholstered leather stools around them. There was a dark wood bar at the far end, manned by two bartenders. The wall behind them was lined with shelves, fully stocked with bottles of Chambers No. 9 and the original Chambers gin. The space over-looked the actual distillery, separated by a massive glass wall. Joanna pointed out the enormous metal tanks on the other side and a pair of large, unusual copper stills Marcus had reportedly sought out at an auction and paid a pretty penny for. Fifty-pound bags of the nine botanicals needed to make No. 9 were everywhere—dried orange peel, coriander and, of course, juniper berries, the essential ingredient in gin.

"Thank you so much for doing this for us," Joanna said. "Marcus and I really appreciate it. I'm glad he's stopped being so daft about you."

"I'm sorry?"

She shook her head. "He's had a thing for you from the day he moved into that building. I'm just glad he got his head screwed on straight."

Marcus had had a thing for her from the beginning? Was that really true? There had been so many unbelievably rough patches since then. "Part of our problem was our first date. I told him this stupid story about how my ex-boyfriend broke up with me because I wasn't ready to have kids. He stopped liking me for a stretch in there. I figured it had to be about Lila. And I understand. I just wasn't ready to discuss that on our first date."

"He can take it a bit far. You should have seen the hoops he made the nanny jump through. I'm sure it would've been easier for her to get a job with the Secret Service. His protectiveness of Lila is certainly an obstacle, but you seem like a smart woman. Certainly you can figure it out. I mean, if you want to figure it out."

Ashley nodded, computing everything Joanna had said.

"So, do you?" Joanna asked. "Want to figure it out?"

Despite her doubts about herself, about whether she could live up to such a monumental and important role, there was only one answer. "I'd like to try."

"Good, then." She put her arm around Ashley and squeezed her close. "Now let's get to work."

Ashley accompanied Joanna as she made her way from table to table. They chatted with writers, laughed with liquor distributors and enjoyed a cocktail along the way. Servers circulated through the room with hors d'oeuvres. Joanna had two employees start small-group tours after Marcus and Mr. Pruitt had reportedly finished theirs. It all seemed to be going perfectly, but Joanna wouldn't stop checking her watch.

"Marcus should be done by now. It's been nearly an hour since they finished the tour. It'll be a shambles if this doesn't go well. Maybe I should go check on him."

One of Joanna's tour leaders grabbed her arm and whispered something in her ear. "Bloody hell. I'll be there in a minute." She turned back to Ashley. "Do you mind running back to the tasting room and poking your head in to see if Marcus and Mr. Pruitt are getting on alright? See if they need anything?"

"Oh, sure. Of course."

"Now that I think about it, that'll be brilliant. Mr. Pruitt asked me some questions about you earlier. Maybe you can chat him up a bit."

Ashley wasn't sure exactly what they could chat about, but she knew very well how to fake her way through a conversation. She looked over her shoulder. "Back here? Down this hall?"

"Yes. That's the way."

Marcus had heard many stories of just how intimidating Oscar Pruitt could be—stodgy, snooty to a fault, a man of the most discriminating tastes who didn't turn down a chance to tell someone just how above it all he was. Marcus had assumed it was merely his reputation and that the real man would be at least a bit more pleasant. He'd been wrong.

Oscar had asked hundreds of probing questions during the tour, nitpicked about every last thing, tried everything he could to rattle Marcus. It'd been trial by fire, and he hoped to hell he'd come across as unflappable. He'd certainly tried everything he could to appear so.

"Why don't we do the tasting?" Marcus asked, stepping behind the bar back in the private tasting room. *Please. I need a blooming drink.* He set out four snifters, two each. The narrow opening at the top of the glass allowed the fragrance of the botanicals to gather, while the stem would keep the warmth of the taster's hand from affecting the temperature and taste of the gin.

"I think you'll be very impressed with the taste," Marcus said. He didn't enjoy having to sell it, but he had to. His father had been hesitant about Chambers No. 9 and the very notion of an American gin. Mr. Pruitt, being as old-school as they came, had the very same ideas.

"Your father calls it a modern interpretation of an old favorite. He seems to think its bloody brilliant."

A wide smile crossed Marcus's face. His father's approval meant too much to feel anything but happiness. Marcus had made a leap of faith by leaving behind his lucrative career and sinking his own money into the company, but his dad had done even more. He'd allowed his son to tinker with a brand that hadn't changed since 1902.

"Of course, I told your father that I would determine that for myself. But I suppose I appreciate his bias. I always want to support what my children do." Oscar removed a pair of reading glasses from the breast pocket of his suit coat and slid them onto his face, peering down his nose as Marcus opened the first bottle.

A side-by-side tasting was the best way to prove to Oscar that Chambers No. 9 represented a step into the modern age while keeping a firm grasp on the company's history. He filled two glasses with one ounce of the original Chambers, then did the same with the No. 9. He added an ounce of water to each, diluting the alcohol and releasing the aromas. "As I told you during the tour, for No. 9, we've expanded the mix of botanicals from seven to nine. The new additions are caraway and elderflower."

Oscar's vision narrowed in on Marcus, the skepticism so clear, Marcus nearly asked him if he spent his entire life hesitating. He then raised the glass to his lips. "The flavor is indeed interesting. Surprising."

Marcus felt a small measure of relief. Oscar hadn't spit it out.

Oscar then took a sip of the original and nodded at Marcus. "I have to tell you, Chambers. Having the two side by side, I can see what you were going for. It's not my inclination to use the word, but I'd go so far as to call it impressive."

Marcus exhaled. His dad would get the story he'd waited for all this time. "Shall we finish up the interview?"

* * *

Ashley walked down the long hall leading to the private tasting room. The sound of her heels on the polished concrete floor echoed in the space, which was otherwise eerily quiet. At the very end, a small sign hung from the ceiling indicating the room with an arrow. The door was open, but voices stopped her just outside it.

"Please don't speak about her like that, Mr. Pruitt." Marcus's words were polite, but his voice was cutting and surprisingly loud.

"It's a valid question. Are you leaving behind your homeland and your heritage for New York and disposable American culture?"

"That's not what you asked. You asked why I would choose to be associated with a woman like Ms. George, both personally and professionally."

Ashley's heart thundered in her chest, all while the blood drained from her face.

"She's a reality television star," Mr. Pruitt continued. "It seems as though you've cheapened your own image in order to garner success. Frankly, I'm shocked that a family as esteemed as yours would stoop to such lows."

The corners of Ashley's mouth turned down. Was that really what people thought? Or was this guy just a pompous jerk? Her money was on the latter, but it wasn't much of a consolation. Marcus had been so excited about this interview, and it was all going wrong. Because of her. She pressed herself against the wall, right next to the door, listening.

"I can't believe you'd cling to such snobbery," came Marcus's voice, "especially since you live in the US for half of the year. You don't even know her. She's one of the hardest working people I've ever met. She may be on television, but it's not an act. She genuinely loves to match people and find them love, and she's amazing at it. If there's any shame in that, it's of your making."

Emotion welled up inside her—a distinct warmth and fullness in the vicinity of her heart. Marcus admired her for all she did. Even better, he'd stuck up for her.

Mr. Pruitt laughed, but there was no frivolity in the sound. It reeked of condemnation and superiority. "I'd say someone is too henpecked to think for himself."

"That's it!" Marcus yelled. It was so loud, so abrupt, that she held her breath. "Get out, now, or I'll show you out myself."

"You're kicking me out of my own interview? Your father has been hounding us for years to do a story on Chambers Gin, and this is what you do when the time comes? I can't imagine your dad is going to be pleased when he hears about this."

No no no. She closed her eyes, willing Marcus to take a deep breath and calm down. She knew exactly how he got when he was mad, as if he was possessed by his anger.

"My father would expect me to come to a lady's defense. If you can't see the propriety in that, there's no point in an interview."

"Well, then. Ms. George has really done a number on you."

Ashley wasn't sure what she should do, but if she hesitated for even ten more seconds, all would be lost, and she'd come face-to-face with the man who'd just said horrible things about her. A tiny part of her thought she should retreat back down the hall. The rest of her was going to march into that room, save Marcus, and take it like a woman.

A distinct look of surprise crossed Mr. Pruitt's face when she sauntered into the tasting room, swiveling her hips and smiling sweetly.

"Oh, hello. You must be Mr. Pruitt," she leaned forward, letting the dress do some of her bidding. She took his hand, holding it firmly. Even when his demeanor made her a bit ill, there was sweet satisfaction in witnessing his bewilderment. "I'm Ashley George. It's *so* nice to meet you, sir. I've heard so many wonderful things about you." She laid it on with the Southern charm, her accent so saccharine it made Ashley's cheeks hurt. She looked up at Marcus, her smile unflinching.

"Ashley," Marcus said. "Were you just out in the hall?" The pure concern on his face was so endearing. The man could be a handsome pain in the butt, but he had a heart as wide as the sky.

"I was. Not for long," she replied. "I heard Mr. Pruitt say that I've really done a number on you."

Marcus blinked. Mr. Pruitt cleared his throat. Her mind scrambled for a way out of the corner she'd just painted herself into. She didn't want to let Mr.

Pruitt off the hook, but she also wanted to save the interview.

"Which I thought was just the sweetest way to put it," she said, exaggerating her accent and taking a seat next to Oscar at the tasting bar. "Marcus and are I quite taken with each other. There's no doubt about that." She slapped the bar with her hand. "Now let's talk gin. I, for one, could really use a drink."

Fifteen

By the time Oscar Pruitt walked out of that tasting room, Marcus was certain the man had no idea what had hit him. Marcus knew very well that there was no preparing for Hurricane Ashley—she made things happen and all you could do was hold on for dear life. Ultimately, Oscar had been completely won over by her. One minute, Oscar had been spewing venom, and the next minute, he was declaring Ashley the most charming woman he'd ever met, referring to Chambers No. 9 as "simply sublime" and admonishing himself for not being a more regular viewer of *Manhattan Matchmaker*. When he parted, Oscar had gone so far as to assure Marcus that the cover story in *International Spirits* would include one of the most glowing reviews he'd ever written. Ashley had saved Chambers Gin from utter disaster.

More important, she'd saved Marcus from himself, which meant she'd kept him from gravely disappointing his father. In the process, he couldn't think of a time he'd been more turned on by a woman. Because of her performance, her mind-numbing dress and the profound relief of having the interview behind him, he wanted only one thing—her, naked, in his bed.

"I need to get you back to the city, and my apartment, now," he said, collecting his suit jacket.

"But your party..." she started, but he held his finger to her lips. That one touch made his blood circulate wildly and warmly.

"Jo can take care of it. I need to take care of you." He decisively flipped off the light in the tasting room. "Let's get out of here."

They hurried to the limo after Marcus convinced his sister to take the reins for the rest of the night. He loosened his tie as soon as they were on the road. "You were amazing tonight, Ashley. Absolutely amazing. I'm not sure I could say anything to you that could match the performance you just gave." He turned and took her hand, his vision drifting over her. She was so beautiful, inside and out, and hell if she didn't manage to surprise him at every turn.

"I couldn't stand out in the hall and let you ruin your interview because of me. I had to do something."

He rubbed her fingers with his thumb. "But you heard those things he said about you. How did you keep from flying into a rage?"

"People have said far worse things about me."

"But people love you. They adore you."

"Believe me, not everyone loves the Manhattan Matchmaker."

"The Manhattan Matchmaker didn't save me from myself. You did. You walked into the room and faced Oscar's ugly attitude. You turned everything on its head by being yourself." The words were right there on the tip of his tongue, begging to burst forth. But would this be too fast for her? Considering her past with her ex, it might be too soon to tell her that he was falling for her, hard. He was falling in love with every last thing about her.

"I couldn't let you down," she said.

He shook his head. "I can't imagine you letting me down." His hand went to her jaw and he kissed her softly.

"Are you sure you aren't saying all of that because of the dress?"

He laughed quietly. "There might not be much defense for that dress, but I'm sure it's not that." He placed his arm around her shoulders and pulled her closer. She turned into him, wrapping her arm around his waist. She gazed up into his face with those welcoming sable eyes of hers. She made him lose all sense of place when she looked at him like that. He committed every electric flicker in her eyes, every bat of her lashes to memory. Perhaps it was his brain's way of distracting him from the way her presence resonated in his body, with a tremor and a low hum.

She's so incredible. And I'm a goner. His breaths became shallow. There was no way to suck in enough oxygen. Ashley was taking all there was to be had. Staying composed while he had her this close was a titanic task, but he didn't want to start something salacious in the back of a car. He wanted to take her home, take off that dress and make love to her all night long.

The lighter traffic at this late hour made it a quicker trip home. They rushed into the building and onto the elevator. The doors slid closed and Ashley practically flattened Marcus against the wall. "The way you were rubbing the fabric of this dress against my skin was killing me. Did you have to do it for the whole car ride?" She kissed him, tugging on his lower lip with her teeth at the end, drawing a guttural groan from the depths of his throat.

He kissed her back, breathlessly. One hand dragged her dress up the length of her leg, craving the chance to touch her thigh. "Sounds like I'm in trouble." His other hand was at her rib cage, caressing in circles, desperate for the moment he could take off her gown and have both hands all over her breasts.

The elevator ding heralded their arrival on the eleventh floor. Even though the moment he'd been waiting for was hurtling at him, getting Ashley into his bed wasn't happening fast enough. His pants were so tight he wasn't sure how he was still breathing, let alone still upright. He grabbed Ashley's hand and took impossibly long strides to get to his door. He hunched over, fiddling with his key. She rose to her tiptoes, chin nearly on his shoulder, breathing hot air against his ear and driving him insane. Finally the key went in.

He wasted no time sweeping her into his arms, their lips tearing into each other. He turned her in circles, much like he had on the dance floor the night of her party. They twirled through the foyer, into the great room, down the hall as they worked at undressing him first—his tie, jacket and shirt were easily gone, left behind on the floor. He had her dress up around her waist by the time they were in his bedroom. Everything about Ashley had his body primed and hungry. He had to have her, body and soul, now. Heat raged inside him, his erection fierce and insistent.

She raised her arms and he lifted the dress above her head. It felt as though he was revealing his reward, a prize he wanted all for himself. He gathered her wrists in one hand, her arms high, part of the dress bunched up around her hands, part of it draping down her back. Even in the near-dark of his room, her skin had its usual soft glow. He drank in her magnificently round beauty, all woman, all feminine mystique. He backed her to the bed and laid her down, clutching her wrists above her head.

"Are you alright?" he asked, stealing a kiss.

"Perfect," she replied.

He cupped one of her breasts, her velvety skin nearly melting into his hands, conforming to his fingers. Her nipples were an inviting rosy pink, pert and tight and sensitive. Every time his fingers got close to them, her skin flooded with warmth.

He stood. "Don't move. Keep your hands where they are."

She clutched the satin dress in her hands. "Whatever you want."

He shucked his pants and boxers, watching her as she watched him.

"You're magnificent with no clothes on. You know that, right?" she asked.

"I'd say the same thing of you, darling." He'd never craved a woman the way he did her, as if he could spend his lifetime exploring her, unlocking her mysteries, learning and admiring. "Can we keep your shoes on?" He stood with his knees pressed against the side of the bed and lifted her leg, holding her ankle, trailing the back of his other hand along her inner thigh.

"You do realize they pinch my toes, right?"

"They do?" he frowned. *Damn. Next time.* "We can't have that." He undid the tiny silver buckle and removed the shoe, placing it on the floor. He did the same with her other foot, then stretched out beside her.

"I want to touch you," she said, raising her head and craning her neck as if she was reaching for him with her lips. "Can I move my hands yet?"

He rubbed her stomach. The parts of him driven by testosterone wanted her hands all over him. But his brain wanted her under his control for a few more minutes. "Not yet."

* * *

Ashley's heart was in her throat. Marcus was so hot when he was like this—taking charge, even bossing her around a little bit. It was probably why she'd never completely written him off when they'd had their spats.

His hand went under the waistband of her black satin panties, but his eyes stayed glued to hers. With every passing second, with every pump of blood through her body, he further occupied her heart. He could have had absolutely anything from her at that moment. Absolutely anything.

Now that she was completely naked, both physically and mentally, he shifted above her, planting his knees on the bed between her legs, his hands on either side of her waist. He covered every square inch of her belly with his warm lips, traveling in circles that radiated outward. When he reached her breasts, he gathered his lips around her nipples, sucking, then flickering his tongue against the tight skin. He kissed the tender undersides of her breasts, then the stretch of skin between them. Every subtle thing he did felt so essential to her being, as if he was coaxing her breaths out of her.

He traveled down her midline with his lips, the kisses becoming deeper, longer, wet. She sucked in a sharp breath when he palmed her thighs and spread her legs wide. Then he kissed her apex and the whole world fell away. He took control, exploring her most delicate places with his tongue and lips, with the patience of a man who knew exactly what he was doing.

Her hips bucked off the bed as his tongue traveled in circles. She couldn't stand not to touch him anymore. She tossed the dress aside and dug her hands into his hair. The intensity was building so quickly in her center that she didn't think she could take it much longer. She felt as if she might explode. She was legitimately concerned that if he made her come as hard as she thought she might, she could end up pinning his head on both sides with her knees. "Marcus. I need you. I need you to make love to me."

He took a few more passes, just enough to make her dizzy, then pressed his lips against her lower stomach. She took a deep breath, willing the pleasurable pressure to recede. She wanted this next part to last.

He removed a condom from the bedside drawer.

"Let me do it," she said, scooting to the edge of the bed.

"Gladly." He handed it over, standing before her, a vision of muscle and masculinity—a very happy vision judging by the way he felt in her hands. A low, guttural breath escaped his lips.

She stroked him, watching his reaction as she tightened her grip. Then she switched to a lighter touch, and that seemed to drive him even crazier. Her fingers traveled his length, slowly, carefully. It felt as if he became even harder with every pass. She couldn't fathom how he could take much more, so she opened the foil packet and rolled on the condom.

He lowered his head, cupped the side of her face, and drew her into a deep kiss. It was as if he was drinking in her very being, and she did the same to him, relishing every heavenly sensation of his touch. She eased herself to her back and bracketed his hips with her knees. "I want you, Marcus. Make love to me."

"I need you, Ash. More than you'll probably ever know." He positioned himself at her entrance, still standing, raising her hips off the bed, carefully driving inside as he did.

She went higher, he went deeper and their bodies were fully joined. He cradled her bottom in his hands. She wrapped her legs around his hips, struggling to make sense of how impossibly good he felt. He was so deep it made her light-headed. He increased their pace, making small but powerful thrusts, keeping their bodies as close as possible.

He had her right back where she'd been a few minutes before, poised on the edge of release, her breaths shallow, almost insignificant. His were coming hard and fast, his lips parted, his eyes closed as he seemed lost in a trance of pleasure. She wanted those lips. She wanted his face in her hands when he gave way. She had to have that closeness.

"Kiss me," she gasped, clutching at the sheets, realizing just how close she was to release.

He reached down and slipped his arms around her, pulling her chest to his as he rolled onto the bed until they were facing each other, on their sides. Their lips were on each other, tongues swirling. Marcus bucked his hips against her, thrusting deep, while the angle brought her a perfect friction. Her insides were wound tight, and there wouldn't be much more she could take before she would have to give in.

The peak sprang on her like a tiger attacks its prey, consuming her. Marcus quickly followed with his own release, holding her close, quieting the movements of her hips with his hands. Their breaths slowed, falling into synchrony. She caressed the side of his face, feeling his stubble against her palm, feeling his smile in their kiss. She couldn't think of another place on earth she'd rather be. *I love him.*

If only she could be certain she wouldn't let him down.

Sixteen

Marcus had been half-awake for a while, basking in Ashley's beauty as she slept. He knew exactly how lucky he was to have found her.

Ashley stirred, stretching and arching her back, rolling her head from side to side on the pillow. A narrow sliver of morning sun peeked between the drapes. It was nearly nine thirty. When was the last time he'd slept so late on a Sunday? It certainly hadn't happened since Lila had been born.

He and Ashley had both needed the sleep. They'd taken full advantage of their night together, only drifting off for short spans before one of them would find the other beneath the sheets, hands would rove, lips would touch skin and the glorious cycle would start all over again. They'd fallen together so perfectly and now a day of reckoning was upon them, or at least upon him. Ashley was due to get her apartment back tomorrow. Their experimental coupling had been more than a success—it was a revelation—but it wasn't the full reality, only a partial one.

"Morning," she said sleepily, folding herself into him, resting her head on his chest.

"Good morning."

He caressed her back, kissed the top of her head. Thinking about what might lie ahead filled him with hope—guarded hope, but he'd take what he could get. It had been so long since he'd felt any hope at all about his future, the future of Chambers Gin, or the things that Lila had ahead for her. He wouldn't let her suffer, but some scars were unavoidable, and she would someday understand that her birth mother had chosen not to be there for her, not for the quiet moments like her first step and not for the big ones either—like her first day of school or her first boyfriend, God help him. If there was any justice in the world, Lila would grow up with two loving, adoring parents to soften the blow of the truth.

He counted on Lila's presence to remind him that the world was still a beautiful place. Now he had Ashley to remind him of the same. Something inside him had been awakened, a part of him that he'd thought Elle had robbed him of. He'd let down his guard and love had come rushing in, the exact opposite of what he'd feared.

But there were two pieces of this beautiful puzzle that remained unsolved, and that scared him more than anything from his past. He couldn't reason either thing away. He couldn't think them away or ignore them. Ashley might be perfect for him, but she might not be perfect for Lila—and vice versa. Ashley was skittish about her ability to handle motherhood. There would be no choice but to end his love affair with Ashley if it proved to be a bad match. He would once again be dragged down into the hell he thought he'd never survive the first time.

And then there was her apartment. She was moving forward with her new builder tomorrow, and that meant moving forward with a life that didn't include Marcus or Lila. He was trying so hard to stay calm, to keep things at a pace that she was comfortable with, but it was incredibly difficult. He wanted to race toward happily ever after, not wait and hope that it would all fall in place. That meant it was finally time to come out with the words he could no longer hold back.

"What do you want to do today?" she asked, resting her chin on his chest. She reached up and played with his chest hair then smiled at him.

She froze him in place with that smile, reminding him to take a breath—this was the way he wanted to feel. Right here, right now. She was the one, the real one. He took her hand in his, wishing he had a big fat engagement ring to put on her finger. "Before we make a single plan, I have to tell you something that I should've said days ago."

"Okay…"

The leading tone of her voice suggested he might

be about to scare her off, but he had to keep going, even if his heart was about to pound out of his chest. "I love you."

Her smile rolled back across her face, ushering waves of profound relief for him. "I was starting to wonder if I was going to have to say it first."

"So you're saying?"

She nodded. "I love you, too, Marcus. I love you so much I feel like there are cartoon hearts coming out of my eyes every time I look at you."

He laughed, her words warming him all over. She had such a way of putting things. "I look at you and my view of the entire world is better. Perfect, in fact."

A rush of pink colored her cheeks. "That's so sweet. You're going to make me cry."

"Don't cry. I'd rather make you happy."

She scooted closer and kissed him softly. "You do make me happy. And I have a confession to make. I think I've been falling for you all along."

And to think they'd been on the same page for a while. "I know I have been. And it made me a real prat there for a while. I'm sorry for that, too, but it was frustrating to see you and feel like it wouldn't work." *And would it work? For real? Forever?*

"I wasn't always on my best behavior either. I think we should both forget that chapter and start fresh." She grinned again. She'd always been full of life, but now she showed him a universe of possibilities, a future.

"I couldn't agree more. Which is why I want to call Joanna this morning and ask her to bring Lila home early. I want us to spend the day together. The three of us."

"You do?" There was an edge to her voice that he'd heard before, full of caution.

"Talk to me. Tell me what you're thinking."

She turned onto her side and picked at the blanket with her fingernail. "I'm happy that you finally trust me to be with her, but I'd be lying if I said it didn't make me nervous. I'm not so naive to think the biggest obstacle between us is that easily overcome."

His stomach knotted, but he tried to push past it. Ashley was not Elle. He knew that. Still… Ashley and Lila hadn't spent any time together at all. That had seemed like the prudent, protective thing to do, but he'd never expected he would fall so head over heels in love. Now he regretted that he'd done things that way, but he couldn't undo any of it. He had to give fate a nudge and hope that things would work out. It wouldn't be Ashley's fault if it didn't work out. She'd never asked to become Lila's mum.

"I don't want you to worry about it. It'll just be the three of us spending a Sunday together."

She nodded slowly, but he could tell that the gears in her head were turning quickly. She was running away with thoughts of where this all went, and that was usually the moment when she started to panic. Precisely the reason he couldn't bring up things like commitment, marriage or dismissing her new contractor.

"And then what?" she asked. "I can't escape the feeling that this is a test, Marcus. What if we don't hit it off? Then what? You tell me goodbye and I have to live across the hall from the man I love but can't actually have?"

"Now you understand exactly how complicated my situation has been all along."

"I always understood your situation. But I need you to see it differently or it's always going to feel like I'm the outsider trying to find her place. Any hesitation from me isn't about a fear of motherhood or responsibility, although I readily own up to both of those things. I can push past that. What scares me so much is that I can't hurt you the way Elle hurt you. It would kill me to disappoint you like that. And then we'd both be heartbroken."

He closed his eyes and kneaded his forehead. Moving forward with his plan was the only way to know. He and Ashley couldn't hole up in his apartment forever. The world outside was still going round. Life was moving ahead. They needed to do the same. It was the only way to get what he truly wanted—a life with Ashley.

"I love that you love me enough to not want to break my heart. But I can't fall out of love with you, Ashley. We can't undo what's been done. The only path for us is forward."

She nodded. "Okay. Call Joanna. Let's bring Lila home."

Ashley was a messy tangle of nerves when the knock at the door came, announcing Lila and Joanna's arrival.

"They're here." Marcus, dressed in his weekend attire of jeans and a T-shirt, rushed over to let them in.

"Hi, hi, hi," Lila muttered in her sweet voice, practically launching herself out of Joanna's arms to get to Marcus.

"There's my girl." Marcus pulled her to his chest, bundling her in his arms.

Ashley wasn't sure she'd ever seen so much pure love between a parent and a child before. He rubbed her nose with his, just like the picture on the bedside table in his room. They both laughed—Lila's were squeaks and giggles. Marcus's were low and came square from his chest, in the vicinity of his heart if she had to wager a guess. Tears welled in Ashley's eyes. It felt as if she was tampering with perfection even to be here. Was she good enough to be such a big part of their lives? Was she worthy of even a second with Marcus and Lila? He'd been so concerned all along with giving Lila the perfect life, but he'd done precisely that. Lila had a daddy who would do anything to protect her and keep her happy.

Ashley's eyes connected with Joanna, who'd been witnessing the reunion and was similarly choked up. Their conversation at the distillery was fresh in her mind, the simplest of questions—*do you want to figure it out?* The answer was an unequivocal yes, even if the prospects scared the living daylights out of her.

"I'm going to run and let you three have your day," Joanna said. She kissed Lila on the cheek. "I'll see you soon, sweet girl." She then ruffled Marcus's hair into a mess. "Don't be a tosser."

"What's that supposed to mean?"

"You know. Have fun today. The three of you. Together." She winked at Ashley and disappeared through the door.

Marcus walked the baby over and stood hip to hip with Ashley. "This is Ashley," he said to Lila. "I want you two to spend lots of time together. Lots and lots of time."

Lila was having nothing of the introduction. She seemed to catch sight of her basket of toys in the living room, pointing and kicking to get down. Marcus was quickly flustered, holding on to Lila while she clearly wanted to play.

"It's okay," Ashley said. "We can't force this."

Marcus walked Lila over to the toys and set her down. The little girl pulled herself to standing with the help of the basket and began yanking toys out of it, one by one, and dropping them to the floor.

"She likes to unpack." Marcus sat down on the floor, leaning against the wall.

Lila's work-like approach brought a smile to Ashley's face. Ashley sat down next to the basket and pulled out a stuffed frog. "Who's this?"

Lila looked at her, holding on to the basket for balance, a deeply serious look crossing her face. She plucked the animal from Ashley's hand and deposited it in the pile with the other toys.

"So that's how this game works?" Ashley reached into the basket again, pulling out a squishy ball and presenting it to Lila. Lila was less concerned now, simply taking the toy and adding to the pile.

"Yes. We put every last toy on the floor and then we play. Not before then," Marcus said. "Lila's rules. I simply follow orders."

"You have Daddy trained. Smart girl." Ashley tried again, finding a well-loved stuffed bunny. Lila's face lit up when Ashley handed it over.

"Oh. Look, Lila," Marcus said. "Ashley found Mr. Bunny."

Lila set Mr. Bunny on the floor, but separated from the other toys, and went back to work, reaching down deep into the basket.

Marcus reached out and held on to the back of Lila's shirt. "This was always my worry, that she'd go headfirst into the basket. It gets a bit treacherous when we get to the bottom."

Lila squirmed against Marcus's grip and let go of the basket, dropping down to sit on the floor.

"What if we just do this?" Ashley grabbed the basket and dumped the remaining toys onto the floor.

Lila's eyes were wide with shock. She stared at Ashley, not moving. Ashley was duly mortified, bracing for a bout of tears. Then the little girl's face lit up with delight. She giggled so hard her shoulders bounced. She scrambled to her hands and knees, crawled to the pile of toys, picked up a block and passed it to Ashley, who wasn't sure what she was supposed to do. So she put it back in the basket. Lila laughed again and went for another toy.

Marcus sat back and shook his head, smiling. "Leave it to you to devise a new game."

"I'm just following her cues," Ashley said, tossing toys into the basket. Once it was filled, she sent the toys crashing to the floor. Lila nearly exploded with fits of laughter.

Marcus joined in, and they played the new game for a good hour until Lila eventually got tired of it and began crawling around the apartment. He and Ashley followed the baby as she explored. She'd pull herself up to standing next to the couch or coffee table, stepping side to side, holding on. At one point she let go of the couch, reached for the coffee table and made the short journey.

"She's going to be walking soon," Ashley said. "Like, really soon."

"I know. It's all going so fast." Marcus sat down on the couch and patted the cushion next to him. "Sit. You should pace yourself."

"I'm starting to get that idea."

He put his arm around Ashley and pulled her close, kissing her forehead. Lila took notice and turned back to them, planting her hands on Marcus's knees and bouncing on her toes. "Do you want up?" He let go of Ashley and scooped Lila up into his arms, planting her on his lap, facing him.

Lila slumped against him, resting the side of her face against his chest, looking at Ashley. Her big brown eyes took everything in—studying, appraising, nothing judgmental. Just collecting data.

Ashley took Lila's hand, the same dimpled fingers that loved to rub her Daddy's stubble. Her skin was so pristine, no signs of age, so fresh and new. Innocent. How could her mother have left these tiny hands behind? How could she have walked away from this sweet face? Perhaps that only underscored what pain Elle must have been in. And could Ashley ever fill the void that was left behind? Or would she spend her days feeling as though she would never measure up?

"I see why you're so protective of her. I see why you only want to hold on to her and never let her go. I can see why you didn't want me within five hundred feet of her."

"Please tell me that you know I don't feel like that anymore. More than anything, I want you to spend time with her. I'm hoping you'll fall in love with her the way you fell in love with me."

Ashley smiled and snuggled up to him on the couch. How could she not fall in love with Lila? Just a few hours with her and Lila had already made herself at home in Ashley's heart. Right alongside her dad.

Seventeen

Monday morning had arrived and Ashley couldn't have been any more sad and conflicted. Her heart felt as though it weighed five hundred pounds. Today was the day she got her apartment back, the day the real cleanup would start, the day her new builder would set in motion the thing that had brought her and Marcus together. She now worried it might tear them apart.

Today was supposed to be a sign of setting things back on the right track, but she knew very well that pursuing things with her apartment was wrong. She belonged with Marcus and Lila. But she'd also put down a ten-thousand-dollar deposit with her new builder. That was an awful lot of money to walk away from when everything was still so new with Marcus.

Considering everything she'd come from, and every-thing her parents counted on her for, she couldn't say that it didn't matter. It did matter. A lot.

All day Sunday, she'd waited for Marcus to insert his opinion on the matter. He was never shy with what he wanted. So where did that leave her? They'd had a wonderful day yesterday, and she really hadn't wanted to ruin it. Now she wished she'd provoked it out of him.

Marcus came into the kitchen and blew out a breath, Lila in his arms. "The nanny just called, and her mother had a gall bladder attack. She's on her way to the hospital right now. Her mother might have to have surgery."

Ashley covered her mouth. "That's awful. Is she going to be okay?"

"They think so, but needless to say, I don't have a backup plan for Lila today. Joanna and I both have a full schedule."

"I'll be home all day dealing with the contractor and the apartment, but I'm used to multi-tasking. I'll take her." Ashley reached for Lila. This time the little girl actually went to her. That felt like a major victory.

"Are you sure? It's a big responsibility and you al-ready have a lot on your plate."

She blew out an exasperated breath. "I'll carry her when I need to be next door and we'll otherwise be here. I'll find a way to make it work." She couldn't believe she was selling Marcus on the idea that she could handle it. "And didn't you say that you wanted

Lila and me to spend as much time together as possible? We'll do great. Go to work."

"So, starting up with the new builder today. That's a big step."

Ashley glanced at the clock. It was eight thirty. He had to leave for the office any minute. Why did he bring this up now when he could have staged a protest yesterday? "It *is* a big step. Do you care to weigh in on this big step?"

He considered her, his eyes sweeping across her face. "I don't want to talk you into anything. That's been my biggest downfall in the past. I'm not about to repeat that mistake."

"What if I give you a free pass? I'd like to know what you're thinking." *Please. Please let me know what you're thinking.*

"I'm not about to make you nervous or skittish about anything. I'm not going to pressure you. You make the right decision for you, and I'll learn to live with it. I just want you to remember one thing."

"What's that?"

He took her hand. "I love you."

Those words felt like code for *fire your contractor.* "I love you, too, but I really just wish you'd tell me what you want me to do. Do you want me to fire my builder? Put the project on hold?"

He sighed. "I'm serious. It might be difficult for me, but I need you to make this decision on your own." He pecked her on the cheek. "I have to get to the office or I'll be late."

She took in a deep breath. *Ten thousand dollars.* "Okay. I'll call you later."

Marcus left for work, and the fire department handed over her apartment forty minutes later. A cleaning team started immediately after that, airing out the space and getting it ready for construction to begin again. These were all things that had to happen no matter what happened between Marcus and her, but it still felt wrong. Every minute of it felt wrong. Even with ten thousand dollars hanging in the balance, it all ate at her.

Ashley fed Lila a snack of yogurt and graham crackers. Then they emptied the toys out of the basket and put them back in for nearly an hour. These were the sorts of moments she'd worried about, whether Lila would feel comfortable with her, but it was going really well. It was going so well that Ashley knew she couldn't use that as an excuse anymore. She and Lila would be fine if she could bring herself to take on the responsibility.

By two, it was time to meet with her builder. Ashley realized that it was probably a little past Lila's naptime, and she did seem sleepy, so she put the little girl in her crib, turned on the baby monitor and went across the hall to her meeting.

Phil with Koch Construction was waiting for her out in the hall. "Ms. George. It's nice to meet you. Why don't we start by walking through the apartment, and you can tell me what was planned and what didn't quite get done."

Ashley let him in, and they toured her apartment,

working around the cleaning crew who were a buzz of activity. The kitchen was a gut job. No question about that. In the rest of the apartment, most of the flooring would be fine, but the entire apartment would need new drywall. The smoke smell would never come out, not even with a fresh coat of paint. Phil made it clear that other builders might tell her otherwise, but the smoke smell always came back.

They went through the guest room and the powder room, eventually arriving back at Ashley's bedroom. Lila fussed over the baby monitor. The meeting with the builder was important, but an unhappy Lila seemed urgent.

"Phil, I need to go get the baby." She decided it was easier just to call Lila "the baby," not to explain her tenuous arrangement with Marcus. She had to admit that she loved the way it sounded.

Phil shrugged. "You shouldn't dote on a baby too much. They usually just cry themselves back to sleep."

Cry themselves back to sleep. That sounded like hell on earth. One minute of Lila fussing and Ashley was ready to surrender. Sure, she was Jell-O. At least she knew this about herself. "Yeah, well, what can I say? I'm a wimp. I'll be right back."

She dashed across the hall and caught sight of Mr. Bunny as she ran through the living room. She grabbed him, then hurried into Lila's room and scooped her out of the crib. "Are you okay?"

Lila cuddled up into her neck, and Ashley cuddled right back. How could she not? Lila accepted affection with no reservation and she gave it in the same way. It was a wonderful experience, even if Ashley had had only a small dose.

Lila shifted, and Ashley felt something wet on her arm. "Oh no. I forgot to change your diaper before your nap." *I'm such an idiot.* She went through the drawers and got out a clean pair of leggings and the cutest top she could find. "I need to take you shopping. Your father does not have much of a girlish flair for fashion." She handed Mr. Bunny to Lila so she could hold him while Ashley changed her diaper and clothes. She wasn't the fastest in the world, but she'd get the hang of it. Eventually.

Lila on her hip, Ashley returned to Phil and the question of what should be done in the bedroom. The minute she walked through the door and saw the wall, the wall that was adjacent to Marcus's room, it dawned on her exactly what she should do. She didn't need to walk away from ten thousand dollars or from Marcus and Lila. What she really needed to do was have Phil knock down a wall.

Marcus's cell phone rang. It was Ashley.

"Everything okay?"

"Actually, everything's great. But I just met with the builder, and I'm wondering if you can come home early and look at something in my apartment."

Something in her apartment? Was she finally going to do it? Crush him with the news that when left to her own devices, she would continue on the path she'd chosen months ago? "And this is important?"

"Yes. I think you'll be happy with it. Just come home. I mean, come over to my side of home."

His head was pounding on the cab ride home—part headache, part Ashley heartache. Could he really be so lucky that this worked out? Or had he let false hope consume him? He wanted to think he was beyond that by now, but he and Ashley had been through so many ups and downs. It wasn't unreasonable to think there were more downs coming. In fact, it was only logical.

He knocked at her door, which she answered quickly, Lila on her hip. That one look confirmed what he'd hoped for—she was made to be a mom. There was no doubt in his mind about that. He kissed his two favorite people in the world, once again reminding himself to take a deep breath, to let things happen. If she was going to move forward with her apartment, they could always turn around and sell it once he proposed. If she said yes. The most important thing here was that he didn't repeat his past mistakes. He wouldn't push her into what she didn't want.

"Come on," Ashley said. "The thing I want to show you is in the bedroom."

You mean the place you'll be sleeping without me? "I thought your bedroom was done." He came to a dead stop outside her room. He couldn't take another step. He didn't want to face what she was about to say. "If you're going to hurt me, Ashley, just do it now. It just feels like you're throwing your future in my face. This future you're building for yourself, one that only includes me and Lila on the periphery. It's not fair to us. And frankly, I don't think it's fair to you, either, because the truth is that we belong together. I've never been so sure of anything in my entire life."

Ashley stood there, staring at him. "So now you tell me your opinion? Finally?" Lila was still in Ashley's arms, playing with her hair.

"Yes. I tried to keep my opinion to myself and let you make your decision without any involvement from me, but I can't do it. I could give you five hundred reasons why we shouldn't be having this discussion, why you shouldn't be telling me whatever fabulous idea you have for redoing your apartment."

"And let me give you one reason why we should." She curled her finger and bounced Lila on her hip, looking at his little girl. "Don't you think Daddy should stop being such a grump and come with us into the bedroom?"

"Da," Lila said, melting his heart. It really did kill him to see how adorable Ashley and Lila were together. If he was already going to be dead, whatever Ashley was about to tell him couldn't kill him any more.

"Okay. Fine." What had Ashley told him hundreds of times? To relax and enjoy himself? He failed to see where the enjoyable part was in this exercise, but he'd go.

"So, here's what I talked about with the builder." She marched to the far corner of her bedroom and smacked the wall. "We start here and we knock down the whole thing, all the way to the other side."

He sputtered. "Ashley. My bedroom is on the other

side of that wall. Where exactly would you presume I sleep during this phase of construction? And why in the world do you want to do that, anyway?"

"It would connect our two apartments. We'd use my bedroom and half of your bedroom and make a larger master bedroom. Then we could enlarge Lila's room. She's going to need more space than she has right now."

His brain sputtered, stopping and starting. Once again, she managed to pull a scenario out of thin air. "Are you saying what I think you're saying? You want to do this?"

"I do. I was standing here with the contractor after I'd put Lila down for a nap. I heard her on the baby monitor, and it felt like my heart was being torn out. I couldn't listen to it for even a minute. The thing that had once seemed more important than anything was far less important than taking care of Lila."

"I'm very familiar with that feeling. It's heartbreaking and wonderful at the same time."

"So I went and got her and changed her diaper. I think that was my mistake. I didn't change her before I put her down for a nap."

"You'll learn these things. All new parents do."

"I'm figuring that out." She smiled, stepping toe-to-toe with him. "You know, I don't like to do things I'm not sure I can be good at. But I realized that this is one thing that nobody ever gets perfect at. I made a mistake, but she was still fine. And she seems perfectly happy."

"I'm looking at her face, and I can tell you that she's more than perfectly happy." He pulled them both into his arms, the two women he couldn't live for even a day without. Ashley hadn't left. She hadn't tried to find a way to slow things down, even though that was her normal inclination. Instead, she'd pushed through it and found a new plan, a perfect plan. A perfect future.

Eighteen

Koch Construction wasted no time once the building board approved the project. Three weeks after Ashley and Marcus had their meeting of the minds in her apartment, the wall between their bedrooms was officially down. She couldn't really believe that Marcus had agreed to something so drastic so quickly, let alone acquiesced to living in a construction zone. When Ashley had asked him about it, he'd said it was all because of love.

"Our bedroom is going to be huge." Marcus shook his head, stepping over the imaginary dividing line between their apartments, a line that was now gone. He smiled, even though the subtext was that he'd bought into one of Ashley's crazy ideas. She could live with that. Plus, he was super sexy in his Saturday attire of jeans and a T-shirt. And to think, they had the entire weekend to look forward to. The three of them.

"A good chunk of it will go to expanding Lila's room. Good thing we have enough space to move everyone around during construction. I really hope my parents will be able to visit once it's all done."

"If they aren't able to come because of your father's health, the three of us will have to make the trip down to South Carolina. It will be good for all of us to get out of the city, and Lila and I haven't seen nearly enough of the US."

Forget impressing her parents with something as frivolous as an apartment. She could show them how well she'd done for herself by introducing them to the stunning, sweet and generous man she'd fallen in love with, and the cutest little girl in creation to boot. "Fresh air. Shrimp and grits," she said.

"Coconut cake?"

"Always."

"Perfect." He put his arm around her and kissed the top of her head. "After that, it'll be your turn to make a trip and come to the UK. Meet my parents. Take a few days away from London and visit the summer house. Rolling green countryside. We can walk to the village every day. It's lovely."

"It sounds it." Really, she couldn't imagine anything better than the grand adventure they had ahead of them. The best part of it was that he was genuinely excited by their future. He seemed to be healing from the pain of the last several years. Grumpy

Marcus was behind him, although he did get touchy about sharing the remote control, especially when *Manhattan Matchmaker* was on. He insisted they watch it every week.

"Maybe by then we'll be engaged," he said, cocking an eyebrow.

She pursed her lips. This was their one sticking point—or, more precisely, it was Ashley's sticking point. Things were happening so fast, and she'd said yes to it all. She'd added to her plate. Heck, she'd gone back for seconds, and it still didn't seem to be enough for Marcus. They couldn't do everything important at one time, could they? "Marcus, you're talking about expanding the distillery."

"We have to up production now that the Hilltop Hotels contract came in. We're talking thousands and thousands of cases of Chambers No. 9 in hundreds of hotel bars."

She sighed. She was happy. Really, she was. She just didn't like the runaway train feeling. "The network just gave me the green light for *First Date in Flight*."

He shook his head. "That right there should tell you just how much the network loves you. I adore you, but it really is a silly idea for a television show. A couple goes on their first date on a cross-country flight? I can't imagine anything worse."

There was a time when this would've prompted a fight, but even she found her own idea a bit ludicrous. Fortunately, at least as far as her career and earning potential were concerned, the network was thrilled. "Believe me. I know."

"You should put Joanna on it." He unleashed a devilish grin.

"I should totally put your sister on that show." Now the wheels were really turning... Maybe she could put Grace on it, too—as the new head of network publicity, Grace had no time for romance. "My point is that our lives are crazy right now. Even crazier than they were a month ago. Do we really want to plan a wedding? I get stressed out just thinking about it."

He pulled her closer and tucked her hair behind her ear. "I don't want you to get stressed. I really don't. But I also don't want to wait to start our lives together."

She pointed at the enormous gaping hole that was once the wall between their bedrooms. "News flash. We've already started."

"I'd still like to get it all sewn up." Quickly he planted a kiss on her forehead. "Lila should be up any minute now. We can go for our walk and talk about it some more."

"Or we could just go on our walk and have fun," she called, but he was already out of the room.

Now that the three of them had been living together for nearly a month, they had routines, one of which was to go for family walks. They would traverse Central Park at Seventy-Second Street near Strawberry Fields, stroll down Fifth Avenue to the southern edge of the park, back across at Fifty-Ninth Street and up again. Lila loved every minute of the sights and sounds of the city, and it was good couple time for Marcus and Ashley. He hadn't been enjoying the city nearly enough.

It was a beautiful May day, almost like summer. Ashley wore a tank top with her jeans, and Lila was in an adorable purple sundress that Ashley had bought for her. The sun shone brightly, the temperatures reaching into the upper seventies. Truly a glorious day in the city. When they arrived at Fifty-Ninth Street, Ashley started veering right, but Marcus walked to the curb with the stroller, waiting for the crosswalk signal.

"Where are you going?" she asked, pointing in their usual direction.

"Let's walk a few more blocks down Fifth Avenue. It's such a beautiful day."

Ashley shrugged and joined him at the light. Two blocks later, she knew precisely what he was up to.

Marcus stopped in front of Tiffany & Co. "Oh. Look where we ended up."

"You planned this. I really don't think it's fair for you to coerce a woman with diamonds."

He leaned down in front of the stroller and lifted Lila out of her seat. "What's that? You think we should go inside and look for a fancy ring for Ashley? That sounds like a splendid idea." He smiled, the sun glinting off his Ray-Bans. "She's so smart. I tell you, I really think we should have her IQ tested. She could be off the charts for all we know."

"You're very funny." She stepped next to him and

pushed his sunglasses down his nose, trying to discern if he really was serious.

He swiped off his sunglasses and hooked them on the front of his T-shirt. "Listen to me, Ash. We're already knocking down walls. Let's knock down the final wall between us. Because the reality is that you've already folded us into your life, and we've done the same to you. We're one unit. A family. We're already here. Let's make it official. It's just a ring. It's not a big deal."

"You realize that's an argument for not bothering, too, right?"

"I do. But I think we owe it to each other. We love each other. We should get married."

"We're talking about a big, expensive party that's going to be a total pain to plan."

"Yes. Exactly. With flowers and a band and a cake and the most beautiful bride in the world."

She looked down at Lila, who was watching the exchange between then. "And how about the most beautiful flower girl, too?"

"We'll have to keep the rose petals out of her mouth."

"We could give her a basket of toys. She'll have no problem emptying it."

He grinned wide. "I like it. Stuffed frogs and Mr. Bunny to step over as you walk down the aisle."

"Do we really want to go ring shopping with Lila? You know she won't be happy in Tiffany. I'm sweaty from our walk. We're both in jeans."

He took her hand. "Ashley George. You and I both

know that we can argue until we're blue in the face, but it's not going to make either of us happy. You're giving me every reason in the book why we shouldn't do this today, but I'd like to give you one why we should."

She had a good idea what he was about to say, but she wanted to hear it. "Okay. Tell me."

"I love you, you love me and we belong together."

She ignored the urge to tell him that he'd actually given three reasons. The truth was that *they* were the three reasons—Ashley, Marcus, Lila. Was there anything else? Absolutely not. Tears rolled down Ashley's cheeks. "Damn you, Marcus Chambers. You made me cry."

"Does that mean yes?"

She looked into those mesmerizing green eyes of his. She couldn't have said no even if she'd wanted to. "That means yes."

"Did you hear that, Lila?" He folded Ashley into his arms and twirled her in a circle, Lila between them. The three of them laughed. "Finally, I win an argument."

* * * * *